My Brother Abe

My Brother Abe

Sally Lincoln's Story

HARRY MAZER

SIMON & SCHUSTER BOOKS FOR YOUNG READERS

NEW YORK   LONDON   TORONTO   SYDNEY

SIMON & SCHUSTER BOOKS FOR YOUNG READERS
An imprint of Simon & Schuster Children's Publishing Division
1230 Avenue of the Americas, New York, New York 10020

Book design by Laurent Linn
The text for this book is set in Arrus BT.
Glossary appears on page 202.

Manufactured in the United States of America
2 4 6 8 10 9 7 5 3 1
Library of Congress Cataloging-in-Publication Data
Mazer, Harry.
My brother Abe / Harry Mazer.—1st ed.
p. cm.
Summary: Forced off their land in Kentucky in 1816, nine-year-old
Sarah Lincoln, known as Sally, and her family, including younger brother
Abe, move to the Indiana frontier.
ISBN-13: 978-1-4169-3884-2 (hardcover)
ISBN-10: 1-4169-3884-2 (hardcover)
1. Lincoln, Sarah, 1807–1828—Childhood and youth—Juvenile fiction.
2. Lincoln, Abraham, 1809–1865—Childhood and youth—Juvenile fiction.
[1. Lincoln, Sarah, 1807–1828—Childhood and youth—Fiction.
2. Lincoln, Abraham, 1809–1865—Childhood and youth—Fiction.
3. Frontier and pioneer life—Indiana—Fiction.
4. Indiana—History—19th century—Fiction.] I. Title.
PZ7.M47397Ab 2009   [Fic]—dc22   2008001106

FIRST
EDITION

For Norma, always

CHAPTER 1

My Little Brother and Me

*W*hen he was three years old and I was five, I learned my little brother his letters, the same letters I had learned from my aunt Betsy. I was taking care of him, while Mama was busy. I showed him the letters in the Bible. "Look here, Abe," I said. "This is an *A*. This is a *B*. This is a *C*. Now you point like I did."

He did it. He pointed to the letters. I didn't have to tell him but once. "Now you're going to make them letters," I said. I was still a little girl and not speaking perfectly. "Come on outside with me," I said. There was nothing to write with, so I made the letters in the air. That puzzled Abe some, and he ran off and found some twigs and gave them to me to make the letters on the ground. "Ain't you smart," I said admiringly.

Three little twigs made the letter *A*. I did it, then he did it. Made it perfect the first time. The letter *B* was harder to make with twigs, so I scratched it in the dirt where the chickens had picked the ground clean. It took him a while to make that *B*, but he was a dogged little squirt. He wouldn't give up for nothing. Then we worked on *C*, and we kept on going, right up the alphabet.

It was funny to watch Abe make the letters, him kneeling on the ground, his butt end up in the air. He'd scratch out a letter with a twig, then talk to it. "*D*?" he said, creaking it out like an old man who couldn't hear so good. "You there, you there? *E, E*, where is *E*?" He loved his letters. "See *C*," he said and laughed at his own joke. *S* was a snake, he said, and *T* was a tree. *Z* gave him some trouble. He kept making it backward. He'd rub it out and do it again, and rub it out and do it again, till he got it right. I learned him to spell his name, too.

Next year, when I was six, Pa signed me up for Mr. Riney's subscription school. Abe was wild to go too. "I'll go with Sally. I will. I will go with my sister," he said, and he wouldn't stop saying it, not even when Pa said, dang it, he didn't have the money. "I will go," Abe said in his little voice. "I will."

Finally, Pa asked the schoolmaster to visit, and Mama and me showed off Abe, showed how he knew his letters and lots more, too. He could already read everything near as good as me. "He can come along with his sister, then," the schoolmaster said. "And I won't charge you extra, Mr. Lincoln, the boy being so young."

I was pleased to have my little brother's company going to school. Pa was pleased to save money. And Mama was pleased that Abe and me were going to get schooling. Mama could read and write. She had come from a fine family, and she wanted us to be educated.

We started school, and every day Abe ran ahead of me all the way on his little legs. It was three miles to the school that sat at the Long Branch crossroads. Abe was the youngest in the school, but he could read and do his letters better than most. I was puffed up over him, proud as a pigeon, which was a sin of pride, but I couldn't help it.

By the time Abe was six, folks were stopping by the house to see the "little wonder"—the child, they said, who could read and write like an angel. They would come with paper for him to write letters for them to family back home in Virginia. Never having had no schooling, most of these people couldn't read what Abe wrote and most signed their names with marks. Pa was a farmer and a carpenter, he could make anything you wanted, and he could sign his name himself, too. He'd stick out his tongue, bite down on it, and slowly make the letters to write *Thomas Lincoln*.

Pa's Knob Creek farm was at the edge of the road.

People walked by all times of the day, and the night, too. Carriages and wagons and drovers went past both ways, and sometimes when the long mule trains came through at night, Pa said it was criminal folks, smugglers. I shivered to hear that, but glad that we were all inside and safe.

In case I forgot to tell you, my name is Sarah Lincoln, but anyone who knows me calls me Sally. I was born on February 10, 1807 in Elizabethtown, Kentucky. My brother was born exactly two years and two days after me at Sinking Spring, Pa's first farm. I don't remember a whole lot about either of those places.

After Abe, when we were living in Knob Creek, Mama had another boy baby. At that time, I was five and Abe was three. That's along about the same time I was teaching him his letters. Mama named the new baby Thomas after Pa. Thomas was a fretful little thing. He died when he was six months old. We buried him right there at Knob Creek. On Sundays, Mama went to his grave and I went with her. Mama had a fine singing voice, and each time she'd sing to my littlest baby brother. "Hush, little baby, don't you cry. . . ." Made *me* want to cry. I didn't, though, not much, anyway. Mama always said that we Lincoln women were strong and we didn't let death nor nothing scorch our eyes.

Did I tell that Abe got his name from Pa's pa, the first Abraham Lincoln? And that I got mine from Mama's cousin Sarah Mitchell? Mama loved her like a sister, and if I asked, she would tell me Sarah Mitchell's story. Something else that made me want to cry. When Sarah Mitchell was nine, she saw her mama cut down by an Indian. Her pa was standing by her mama's body and attempting to hold off the attackers with a rifle he was using like a club. Sarah and her brother were hiding in the bushes, but they were discovered and ran for their lives.

Whenever Mama got to this part of Sarah Mitchell's story, I would get all fearful and trembling. Sarah and her brother ran till they came to a log fallen across a river. Sarah's brother scrambled his way across the log to the other shore and called to her to follow, but she was scared of the water. She hesitated, and the Indians came upon her and took her away.

They held her captive for six years and then they freed her in a prisoner exchange. After that, she went to live with Aunt Betsy and Mama. "And what was that like for Sarah, being with the Indians, Mama?" I would always ask. And Mama would always press her lips together and say, "Sarah vowed they treated her fine, made her part of a family. But I'll tell you, Sally, it was sweet to see her in our house, and we loved each other. We were like two fingers on the same hand. Sister-cousins people called us. I promised I would name my first girl after her. And so I did."

"And so you did," I said, hugging Mama. I couldn't imagine being anybody but Sally Lincoln. Nor could I imagine living anywhere but Knob Creek. I thought we would never leave it.

— CHAPTER 2 —

How Can People Be So Mean?

Everything about our life at Knob Creek was good. We had school in the winter, and in spring when Pa plowed and Abe followed with the seeds, I was with Mama, cooking and making the garden and gathering herbs. Mama was teaching me all the time, correcting me, showing me the right way to do things, like making apple butter and washing clothes and how to peg them on the line so the wind would get them and they'd smell good and fresh.

"When you grow up," she said, "and you get married and have your own family, you'll know how to do everything a girl needs to know."

"But, Mama," I said, "I don't want to get married. I want to stay with you forever. And Abe and Pa too." Mama laughed and said I'd change my mind. "No, Mama, I won't," I said.

"Oh, you will," she said. "I used to be just like you."

I knew Mama was wrong and I was right. I wished I could just say it, but I didn't. It would be sassing.

The fall of the year that I was nine and Abe seven, two peculiar things happened. Pa didn't split wood for the winter and he didn't sign us up for school. "Don't we need wood, Pa?" I asked.

"Never mind," he said.

"But we'll be cold. I don't want to be cold."

Mama shook her head at me and put her finger on her lips, meaning *leave your pa alone*. I obeyed Mama. I didn't pester Pa nor did Abe, but we puzzled about the wood and we mourned not going to school. "Why not?" Abe kept asking me. I didn't know what to say. I heard Pa and Mama talking about lawyers and "faulty surveys" and "ejectment proceedings," but I didn't know what it meant.

Then Pa went away for a week. Mama said it was to look at some "Congress land" up north in the new territory they called Indiana. One evening after Pa came back, he said, "Children. We're going to be leaving this place. This farm ain't mine anymore."

Abe looked up from his book. "What do you mean, Pa?" he asked. "That don't make no sense. This farm is yours."

"No, it ain't," Pa said. "We linger much longer, the sheriff will be here to put us out."

"Mama?" I waited for her to speak, to say it wasn't true. It wasn't for me to speak up to Pa, but then I did anyway. "Pa! We can't leave here. This is our home."

"I don't need you telling me things I know better than you, Sal."

"But, Pa—"

"Quit your jawing. When are you going to start acting like a girl?"

I looked down. A girl was supposed to be modest, dutiful, and quiet. I found that quiet part real hard. Well, maybe I didn't want to be a girl.

Turned out it wasn't just us Lincolns losing our land. Neighbors of ours were losing their farms too. "Your pa and them did things right," Mama said, "bought the land fair and square, but some folks back east, some rich Philadelphia people, have paper that says the land is theirs and we had no right to buy it. All the work your pa has done is gone for nothing."

"That's wrong, Mama!" I said.

"It's the law. The rich gobble up everything. Poor

people like us can't do anything about it. The rich have the lawyers."

"How can people be so mean," I cried out. "I hate them, Mama. I hate them!"

"Hush your mouth. No use in hating," Mama said. "The Lord forgave and we need to forgive. We'll manage, Sally. We'll manage."

CHAPTER 3

Leaving Home

*A*fter Pa told us we had to leave Knob Creek, it didn't take us but a day and a half to strip our cabin bare. We had to leave behind everything Pa had built, starting with our cabin, the fencing around the cleared fields, and the animal enclosures. We didn't have no wagon, so we had to leave our table and beds and stools, too.

Pa said he had a mind to burn the cabin and everything in it down to the ground, but Mama said, "They'll put the law on you, Mr. Lincoln. You know you'll build everything again." Then a neighbor came by and Pa swapped him the table and the four stools, plus the corner cupboard, for a steel plow tip. And after that, there was nothing to do but go.

The day we left, we loaded our horse, Branch, with Pa's tools, the new steel tip, seeds for spring planting, cornmeal and meat for the trip, and Mama's wheel and pots. All of us carried something, but when Pa saw me packing the smooth, shiny stones I'd collected, he told me to leave them. "There's stones aplenty where we're going," he said.

I was afeared he'd tell me the same thing about Amanda, my corn-husk doll that Mama had made for me when I was little. I had her tied to my waist. I flung the stones away, but no matter what Pa said, I wasn't going to leave Amanda.

CHAPTER 4

On the Road

T left Knob Creek with a heavy heart and a slow foot, still hoping that Pa would stop and turn back and say that he'd changed his mind. But he started out brisk and kept moving, almost hidden under the pack on his back. We all carried packs, Mama's was on her shoulders attached to a tumpline. She was leading Branch, who bore the biggest load.

The day was gray and gloomy, not a speck of sun in sight. It had rained during the night and the road was rutted and muddy. Abe and I were barefoot and at every step red mud grabbed our feet. Abe thought that sound was funny and made a big thing of taking giant noisy steps.

The road ran through woods and then cleared land and then more woods. We were never alone for long. We passed farms and cabins with smoke coming from the chimneys, and travelers on foot and in wagons going by in both directions. Abe and me dawdled to look at the men on horseback, and the people riding in carts and the folks on foot, with their goods piled up, pulling the carts themselves.

Pa turned and signaled for us to step along. "I'll race you, Sal," Abe said. He started off running, lifting his legs high and splashing down into the mud. "Come on, Sal! What's the matter?" I weren't about to get covered with mud, but Abe kept running, and he was soon out of sight. Mama and Pa were out of sight too. I was alone.

I stopped and slipped the pack loose and sat down near an oak tree. At my waist, Amanda looked up at me with her pinprick black eyes. *What are you doing, Sally?*

"I'm taking a rest."

Well, nobody else is.

"I'm not nobody else. I guess you must have noticed that."

Your pa don't care about any of that stuff. Where he goes, you go.

"My feet hurt."

Awwwww, poor little Sally.

"I'm not faking it!"

You better go, Sally, and catch up with them.

"When I'm ready, I'll go, Amanda. Now, be quiet!" I turned her so her face was against my waist.

For a while, I watched the traffic. The road was wide and it looked like everybody in the world was going someplace. A wagon pulled by oxen and loaded with sacks of corn went creaking by. Then more wagons, some with families like ours, only with more young 'uns, and drovers with herds of pigs and sheep and cows and strings of horses. It was a real merriment watching all this.

A stagecoach behind six galloping horses overtook everyone, crowding them off the road. Those horses splattered mud in every direction. I scrambled back and wiped at the mud on my dress. Faces in the coach window, big red faces, were looking out and laughing at me, as if this was good sport. I hated them. They were rich people, same as the ones who had taken our farm.

I snugged on my pack, turned Amanda around, and started walking again, expecting to see Mama and Pa. I walked faster and faster, and they weren't anywhere in sight. "Amanda, why didn't they wait for me?"

Why didn't you stay with them, Sally?

"Because I was tired and needed a rest! You know that. Do you think they forgot me?"

No, I don't think so, Sally. Oh, look! Here comes your brother.

Abe slid into place alongside of me. "Pa says you better hurry. He says if I can keep pace, you should too."

"Your legs are longer," I said. The bottom half of Abe had been growing, and he was as tall as me.

"Don't matter. Pa's mad."

"Well, I'm mad too. I'm mad at those rich people."

Mama and Pa were waiting for us at the schoolhouse crossing. "What's wrong with you, Sally?" Pa put his hand on my shoulder. It lay there like a stack of wood. "Are we going to have trouble with you?" I shook my head. "Let's go, then."

We didn't stop again until midday when Mama said, "Enough, Mr. Lincoln," and called a halt for food. If she hadn't spoken up, Pa would have walked us all through the day and the night, too. He was like a mule, nothing stopped him—wet, cold, muddy, windy, he didn't care.

As dark came on, I was hoping that Pa would ask for shelter at a cabin, but no. He led us off the road and into the woods. We stopped in a clearing by a stream and made camp. Abe and me gathered wood for a fire and hemlock boughs for the bed. We set ourselves around the fire and Mama sang grace. "Thankee, Lord, for this food and my children and for keeping us all safe." After we ate, she threw our bear skin across the hemlock and we all lay down and pulled our feather quilt over us.

The next day was just like the first day. Walk, walk, walk. That night we came to an inn where the wagon drivers and the drovers stopped. "Pa! We can sleep in there," Abe said. All around the inn were pens and corrals and fenced areas for the horses and sheep and pigs.

"I ain't sleeping in a room full of drunken men," Pa said. "And neither are you. And we're not letting your mama and sister in that place, that's for sure." Again, we made camp in the woods.

Pa was in high spirits the next morning as we started off. "We're going to the promised land," he sang. "Good sweet land, full of streams and meadows."

My shoulders ached and I was missing being inside four walls. I just wanted to get where we were going, and I didn't care if it was the promised land or the ends of the earth. "Ask Pa how much more walking we got to do," I told Abe. I'd already asked Pa about ten times, and each time he said, "We'll be there by and by."

"I don't want to ask Pa," Abe said.

"Why not?" But I knew. Pa always had a sharp answer for Abe.

That night, we were all sitting around the fire when Pa said, "We cross the river tomorrow."

"Then we're there, Sal!" Abe said. He jumped up on a stump and started talking like a preacher. "We're on our new land; it's got fish in the creek this big." He stretched his arms. "No, this big." He stretched his arms even farther. "And there's a salt lick and game comes there from every direction, ain't I right, Pa? And birds, so many you just knock them out of the trees, bang, bang, bang, ain't that right, Pa?"

"Keep talking," Pa said. "That mouth of yours sure can go. If you could talk us there, we'd be there right now."

Abe got off the stump and started throwing bits of sticks and grass into the fire. Mama called him over to her and put her arm around him. I wished Pa wouldn't be so sharp to Abe. Pa said sharp things to me, too, but I didn't take it so hard, not the way Abe did. 'Course, I knew Pa favored me. Maybe that was a sin of pride, thinking I was special.

CHAPTER 5

The River Shone Like Silver

As we came up onto a bluff, I saw the river spread out below us. It was huge. It shone like pure silver. Then we were back on the road again and cutting fast through the trees down the trail to the river. The closer we came, the bigger the river got. I could hardly see across to the Indiana side. There sure was no stepping across, the way we stepped across our creek. I hugged my brother tight and we both stood there and marveled at the wonder.

"Look at all them boats," Abe said.

We gaped at the sight: boats and barges, dugouts and canoes thick on the water. But Pa had no time to linger and marched us down to the shore. Where we stopped was a tangle of roots and snagged trees. We dropped our packs and unloaded Branch so he could drink.

Pa went off to the landing to wait for Mr. Thompson who he knew from having been here before. That time was when he went over to the Indiana side.

"You young 'uns clean up good, now," Mama said. "Get that mud off your feet." She went up the hill to have a chat with the ferryman's wife.

I got down on my hands and knees and splashed my face and drank, but when I put my feet in the river, the water was so cold I jumped right out. Abe laughed at me and went in and splashed around till his feet turned white and nearly froze. Then I saw the ferry coming across from the other shore, and I started in waving. The water was moving so fast I was afeared the ferry would be washed downriver, right past the landing where Pa was waiting.

Abe got hold of a chunk of wood. "Watch this, Sally," he said. "Watch me sail this across the river."

"Never!" I said.

He heaved it out, and it was washed away in a moment. "Chuck me a stone," he said. I found him a stone, and he threw it. Anybody could see he'd never make it even halfway across the river, but he wouldn't stop trying. He kept throwing stones and climbing out farther and farther on the tangle of trees and brush along the shoreline.

"Abe, get back here," I yelled. "I'm going to let you drown if you don't get back here this minute." He paid me no mind. Then Mama and the ferryman's wife and two boys came down the hill.

"Where's your brother?" Mama asked. I pointed to where Abe was standing on a half-drowned log. "Abraham," Mama said. "I need you here by me." She barely raised her voice, but his head came up, and he was back in a flash. That was always the way. I could yell myself hoarse at him, but Mama only had to say his name and he'd be there.

"These are my children," Mama said to Mrs. Thompson. "They both can read and write."

"God bless them," Mrs. Thompson said. She was a round little woman. "Now, my boys can't read much, but they're a great help to their father. Boys, get ready! Your pa is coming across."

The two Thompson boys were eyeing us. "Let's see him do some writing," the older one said. He was near about my age.

"What do you want me to write?" Abe said.

"You should know, you're so smart."

Abe went down on one knee and scratched out two words in the dirt.

"What's that?" the Thompson boy said.

"Ohio River," Abe said, squatting back on his heels.

"'Taint," the boy said. "That's the river there. Anybody knows that."

"It's the *word* for the river," I said. "The river is the river, and the word is the word."

"Huh!" the boy said. "What's your name?"

"I'm Sarah Lincoln, and this is my brother, Abraham."

"Well, my name is John Thompson, and what do you think of that? Pretty soon I'm going to be a ferryboat captain like my pa."

"Lookee here, John Thompson," Abe said, and he scratched John's name in the dirt. "That be your name. It's not you. You're you, and that's the word that's your name."

John studied the letters. "Ain't that something," he said at last.

"You can do it same as me," Abe said. "I'll learn you. That little hook is a *J*. You could put your coat on it. Then you got an *o*, like a wagon wheel, *h* is a chair, and then all you got to do is *n*, and that's like a two-legged stool."

"Couldn't sit on it," John said. He jabbed his brother. "There's Pa coming," he said, and they ran off.

"Let's go," I said to Abe, and we ran after them down to the landing. The men on the ferry poled toward shore. It were a great sight to see! One of them threw a rope, and that boy John stepped into the water and caught it and tossed it to his brother, who snagged it around a stump. Then they did the same on the other side, and after that they climbed up on the boat and worked together with the men to pull it up tight against the landing.

I studied that ferry. It was flat and seemed to float on top of the water like a leaf. It was an amazement to me that it was safe and didn't sink with all the folks and animals on it. The people who'd come across from the other shore started unloading their wagons and horses and goods. I could have stood there and watched and never moved, it was so remarkable.

"Sally!" Pa called me to attention. It was our turn to load on. The Thompson boys helped us. Pa led Branch on and tied him up to a post in the middle.

"Good-bye," Mrs. Thompson called to Mama, and Mama waved as the ferry broke free from its mooring. We were moving! The ferry rocked. Branch snorted and stamped.

"He don't like being on the water," Pa said and hobbled him good. Then he went in back to talk with Mr. Thompson, who was steering.

I stood close to Branch and rubbed his neck and talked to him. "We're not going to sink," I said, but I weren't so sure. Mama was sitting nearby on our bundles, resting herself. She had her eyes closed. Abe was all over the boat, looking at everything. He went right to the edge. "Abe," I yelled, "you're going to fall in and get swept away." He paid me no mind. Next, he was talking to the oarsmen on the sweep. He grabbed ahold of an oar and stroked with them.

"Stand back, boy," one of the men said.

I got ahold of Abe's arm and hung on to him. "Look here," I said, "we're standing on top of the river. Ain't that grand! And look at that sky! Did you ever see anything so big?"

"Pa could clear a hundred fields, and it wouldn't be nothing to that sky," he said.

"I know you're right!" For the first time I was almost glad we'd left Knob Creek, glad for me to see such wonders, this vast river and the sky so big.

CHAPTER 6

On the Far Shore

On the ferry, we didn't have to carry nothing, we didn't have to do nothing, and if we'd only been going where the river went, we could have sat and jawed till we reached the Mississippi. But once we got off the ferry on the other shore, the river and the wonder of it was soon behind us. We loaded up Branch, shouldered our sacks, and started off again. The road climbed away from the shore and curled into the gloom of the forest.

This Indiana side didn't seem near as civilized as Kentucky. The road wasn't near as good as the road that had gone past our farm. It was narrow and rutted from all the wagons coming through. The people were mostly families like ours, some with packs on their backs like us, but others with wagons and carts hauled by mules and horses and oxen.

We passed wagons slowly struggling uphill, and we passed wagons broke down and stuck, and people sitting by the side of the road. Pa didn't look left or right. He just kept going. He was ahead of all of us, setting a steady pace. Abe ran to catch up, and for a while it was him and Pa up front, and me and Mama behind.

"Sally, we should have put a rope on those two," Mama said. She had dozed off on the boat, and it had set her up fine. "They'll get so far away, they'll forget about us."

"I wouldn't mind losing them two, Mama," I joked back. "Just you and me, we could find us a nice little shack and move in."

Right then, as I said it, we passed another farm with a field full of stumps and the people living in a shack that didn't look like nothing more than a pile of wood with a chimney.

"Oh no," Mama said. "I don't want to live in a shack. I grew up in a nice home, Sally. We had chairs with backs and a cupboard full of dishes, and we each had our own fork and knife, and my uncle had two slaves who did all the hauling."

I thought about that for a while, then I said, "Pa hates slavery, Mama. He says it takes the bread away from free men like him."

"I know," Mama said. "I feel the same way. It's ungodly.

Where we're going, there is no slavery, and your pa and I are both real glad about that."

What Pa finally called a halt, we set ourselves down by a big rock split by a tree growing right out of the center of it. We sat on the ground and Mama got out the food. Mama sang grace, and then we set to eating. "How much farther we got to go, Pa?" I asked.

Mama gave me a look, but Pa he was nice and said we'd come halfway already. "Near fifty miles we got behind us. Thirty miles more to the trace. Two days should put us there."

Just knowing we were halfway to the end made my pack feel lighter. When we started out again, Abe and I raced each other, and we even got ahead of Pa for a while. Later, we slowed down and walked along with a family that didn't even have a horse, nothing but a brew of young 'uns, each of them carrying something. I never got the number of them right.

"We're from back east," one of the boys said.

And his brother—older, looked like—put in, "We been walking all the way from Virginia."

"That's right," the man said. "We're on the way to the promised land." He was talking to Pa. "We never owned nothing. I hired out all my life, hired out my brood, too, and what do I have to show for it? Nothing! Work a plow for another man, you might as well be an ox."

Mama called me over to admire the baby. A girl, same age as me, was holding the child on her hip. She had a rope of hair down her back same as me, except hers was light and mine was dark, and her name was Sarah, just like mine. If we didn't both carry the same name, we could have been sisters.

"Hello, Sally Sarah," she said.

"Hello, Sally Sarah," I said.

"Hello, Sal," she said.

"Hello, Seal," I said, and we both laughed. The baby grabbed her hair and put it into his mouth, and we laughed harder. We had good fun for a while, then her pa called a halt, and we went ahead.

Later that afternoon, Pa came across folks he knew from back home, two brothers named Jones, and their wives and young 'uns. Their covered wagon was stuck. It was a pretty wagon, painted red, with big tree rounds for wheels. They had broke an axle and didn't have another and no tools, either.

Pa had the tools. I was real proud of the way he knew just what to do. He picked out the oak tree he wanted cut and shaped a straight length of it into a new axle. Everyone watched him and Abe, who was bringing Pa the tools he needed. Then all of us, every living soul except the baby, set to unloading the wagon and raising it up, so Pa could set the axle in place. When it was done and the wheels were back on, the Joneses gave three cheers for Pa.

Mrs. Jones said, "You folks are staying and eating with us."

I looked at Pa, hoping he'd agree, but before he could even say anything, Mama said, "Thankee! We'll be pleased to do that."

I went with Mama to help with the food and the fire. That was a good meal! We ate meat and corn pone, and it was a lively time. Darkness came. Me and the other girls were rhyming, the mamas were talking together, the boys were off wrestling, and Pa was with the men, smoking his pipe and passing the jug around. The men's voices got louder and louder.

"I got eighty marked acres I mean to keep," Pa said. He stood up and walked all around the fire. "Congress land. Any man who comes and says he's got prior claim, I'll spit in his eye."

"Nobody's gonna take it from you, Mr. Lincoln," Mama said. She got up and took a tug on Pa's pipe. "God wants you to have that land."

"Amen!" the other mamas said.

Then my mama started the singing with her fine voice.

"Praise our God. O, praise be given." When Mama sang, it was as good as anything in the world. I sang with her, Pa joined in, and then all the other people. If only it could be like this all the time, I thought, us among other folks, the singing and the fire crackling, and all above the silent stars.

☙~ C H A P T E R 7 ~☙

The Trace

℟ound midmorning the next day, Pa found where he'd left his initials blazed in an oak alongside of the road. He sank his ax into the tree and said, "That's my mark. This is it."

This was what? Was *this* our land? All I could see were trees, a wall of trees, and beyond them, more trees. Trees standing, trees leaning, and trees fallen. Nothing but trees disappearing into the gloom.

"Are we going to live here?" I said.

"This is the trace," Pa said. "We still got sixteen hard miles, so let's get going." He walked into the trees and we followed. A couple of dogs that had been trailing us on the road came along too.

If there was a trail, it wasn't more than an animal track,

a trace that wound this way and that through the trees. Pa had made an ax for Abe to fit his size, and they went ahead, chopping vines and brambles and fallen limbs.

Mama and me followed, clearing enough of a trail for the horse to come through. Brambles scratched and grabbed at me. A bite was in the air, but it might as well have been the middle of the summer, I was so hot and sweaty. I sat down on a fallen tree for a rest and sank right through it. It was all rot and mush and stink. "Mama!" I shrieked.

She came over and studied me. Her hair had come loose, and there was dirt on her face. "You're a sight," she said, as she pulled me up.

"So are you, Mama!" The words were out before I could stop them.

"Sal!" She slapped me. "Don't be insolent. Now, let's get back to work."

That first day we made two miles. Hard miles, like Pa said. I was all scratched up and ready to stop ten times before he called a halt for the day. It was a pretty spot by a stream. The water was tumbling over the rocks and when I looked up, I could see a little bit of sky.

Pa went hunting and took Abe. I gathered up wood, and Mama, using Pa's flint and iron and a piece of tow from her ball of thread, built the fire. She found some greens and cress along the stream, and we had that with johnnycakes and roasted grouse and squirrels. Everything tasted real good. I sucked every bone dry.

We made our bed near the fire. Branch was tethered near us, and the dogs was sleeping close. I cuddled to Mama and lay there looking up at the stars far above. I heard a mad hooting, and then I was asleep.

In the morning, Mama and Pa were up before Abe and me. Mama was heating water on the fire, and I could hear Pa chopping away. That day was like the day before. Hard miles. Some places the trees were burned almost flat or blowed over, like a giant hand had come rolling down over everything.

One place was flooded and so mucky that Abe, who'd gone ahead, sank in almost to his waist. Pa got him under the arms, but then he was sinking too. "Nancy! Sal!" he yelled. "Get over here and help. Drag over some brush. Anything. And don't get stuck yourself."

"Here, Sal, hurry," Mama said. We commenced to drag a big fallen limb over to where Pa and Abe were stuck. They grabbed on to it and crawled out. They were both covered with mud. Once we were clear of the mucky land, Mama wanted to stop, so we could all clean up.

"No," Pa said, "we lost enough time already because of that fool boy. Running off that way! All he wants to do is play."

Abe looked at Pa, his mouth half open.

"Abe ain't playing, Pa," I said. Mama put a finger to her lips, but it was too late. The Devil had my tongue. "He's right there with you, working hard as he can, and you don't ease up on him, and he can't work equal to you, nobody can. And—"

"And nothing, Sal," Pa said, stopping my tongue finally. "I don't need you to tell me nothing. You better look to yourself. You just mind your mother and mind your mouth. I don't say the boy don't work, but if I let up on him, he's off adventuring, and look what that got us."

We all fell in line, Pa and Abe in front, opening the trail. After that severe chastisement from Pa, I was feeling real tired. I kept looking at Mama, but she didn't say nothing either. Branches slapped me in the face and vines tripped me up. It was like Pa was punishing me, and I knew I deserved it. I got poked in the eye and cried out, "Mama!" For a moment, I thought she wouldn't even look at the hurt. "It's my eye," I moaned. "I got something in it."

Mama rolled up my eyelid. "It's a scratch," she said. "It'll heal." She patted my head, then she put her arms around me and said, "Don't fret, Sally. It'll pass. The Lord will provide."

After that, even though my eye kept on hurting, I worked with a better will.

The next day it was raining without letup, and the

wind was blowing hard. I was wet right down to my skin. "Keep moving," Pa said. I was shivering when I spotted an opening in a hill. It was like a cave, and there was just enough room for us all to crawl in and sit huddled together. It was full of foul animal smell. I supposed a panther lived there.

"Bear," Abe said.

"Panther," I said.

"Bear!"

Pa patted his rifle. "Whoever he is, if he comes home, we'll invite him to dinner."

Pa made a fire, and Mama got out the quilt and wrapped up Abe and me and put our clothes to dry. The dogs kept trying to come in with us, and Pa kept driving them out. We slept there that night. For a long time I listened for the animal that owned this cave. The rain fell steady and hard. Sometimes it sounded like footsteps, but the dogs were lying in the opening now, and I was real glad for them.

The next day, it weren't raining, but the wind was still blowing. Midday, we were pushing through dry canebrake growing high over our heads. It was choking in those reeds. With Mama ahead of me, I couldn't see nothing, and all I could hear was the rattling sound they made. I was never so glad as when we were clear of them.

We were all chopping and clearing the path when Pa stopped and said, "We're here!" I didn't know what he meant. I couldn't see nothing much different from what I'd seen before. Trees, trees, and more trees. "This is ours," Pa said. "Our land. Ain't it grand!"

═══ CHAPTER 8 ═══

The Fearful Quiet

The journey was over, but what had we come to? I looked down under my bare feet, and I couldn't see nothing much different from where I'd stepped a minute before, and a day before, and the day before that. I must have been dreaming that our Knob Creek cabin would be here waiting for us, and we'd have walls around us and a fire to warm by. And since I was dreaming, guess I dreamed us a high road nearby with the creaking wagons and the clomp of horses and grunting of pigs, and the muffled voices of men and sometimes the quickening in the air of a snapping whip.

But that was someplace else, not here. Nothing like that here. Nothing at all here. Nothing but trees. I was cold and wet. We were alone in this forest, with all these giant trees. It was fearful quiet.

Maybe we weren't meant to stay here. One of Mama's cousins lived somewhere nearby and Pa's uncle was somewhere by too. Maybe we were only stopping to rest, and then we'd move on to a relative's place and stay there while Pa built us a cabin. But I knew better than to ask. When Pa had come here in the fall, he had thrown up a lean-to, three walls and a roof. That was our home now. An open-faced shelter. I tethered Branch to one of the stumps, so he could browse. Then, for a while, we all got in under the shelter and just sat there on our bundles.

Mama prayed. "Thank you, Lord," she said, "for bringing us through the wilderness to our land." Then she waited till she heard Abe and me say it too.

"Thank you, Lord," I said, but my whole heart weren't in it. I was thankful we was off the trace and that we weren't going to sleep in the open tonight, but I couldn't help wishing what we had was better than this.

Nobody was talking a whole lot. Pa was the only one who was the least bit cheerful. "Do you hear that?" he said. Suddenly, something was making an awful racket, sounded like a million locusts all talking at once.

"I hear it," I said.

"I hear it," Abe said.

"You'd be deaf if you didn't," Pa said. "That's pigeons coming down to roost by the creek. Pigeon Creek.

That creek runs clear from our land all the way to the Ohio River."

Pa was eager to go hunting and got the fire going fast, using the fire pan of his gun. "We're never going to let this fire go out, are we," he said.

"No, Pa," we said.

He went off hunting, and Mama got Abe and me going. She gave us the cedar pail and told us to find the spring and bring back water and firewood. Pa had told us the spring was just up the hill. Abe went crashing ahead, so intent on finding the spring before me that he stumbled over rocks and fell. "Serves you," I said, wiping his cheek where he'd bloodied it.

"Ain't nothing but a scratch," he said. He straightened up. "Listen! Do you hear it?" And he was off again. "Found it, Sal," he yelled.

Near the top of the hill, water was oozing out over a rocky outcropping and splashing into a pool. With the bucket full, we started back down. "You carry it," Abe said. "I'm going to find Mama some good dry wood."

I took the pail. "You don't have to run off," I said. "It's all here." There were dead dry branches everywhere.

When we got back, Mama had corncakes going on a stone at the edge of the fire. Pa came back loaded with pigeons, and we roasted them on the coals. Abe had his eye on that stack of birds and I can't say I didn't either but Mama sang grace first. "Praise the Lord. . . ." And then we set to. Everything was delicious, and the dogs had a feast of bones.

That night we lay together in the shelter, Pa with his gun on one side and Mama on the other, and Abe and me in the middle. I had Amanda next to my face. There was ice in the air, and I stuck my head under the quilt, but Pa had set a night log to smoldering, and my feet, closest to the fire, were tingling warm. Everyone was sleeping but me and Amanda—Pa snorting like he was arguing or fighting, Abe breathing regular like the creak of leather, and Mama's breath so soft, I was afraid she'd stopped breathing.

"Mama," I said. "Mama."

"Hush, Sally," she whispered. "I was just dreaming about our Knob Creek farm."

"I wish we were there, Mama. Pa took us away."

"You know that's not so." The sleep went out of Mama's voice, and she pulled my ear. "That's wicked talk. We were driven off the farm. Don't you forget that. Just be thankful God gave your father the strength and wisdom to bring us here."

"Yes, Mama."

Outside, there was an awful stillness, not a human sound. I heard an owl, *hoo, hoo, hoohoohoo*, and another owl answering, then sharp high yips that could have been a wolf or coyote, or savages signaling back and forth as they crept close to where we slept.

Dear God, I prayed, *I know I'm wicked, I know I'm not worthy, but if You'll protect us, I promise I'll try harder to be an obedient daughter. Dear God, hear my prayers and please don't turn Your eye away from us.* Then, holding Amanda close, I fell asleep.

CHAPTER 9

We Are Not Alone

"Sally!" Mama's voice found me huddled under the quilt. It was a week now that we'd been here, on our own land. Snowflakes, silent and light as goose down, filled the air and drifted into the lean-to. Snow was in my hair, tickling my lips, and lay like a soft blanket over the quilt. I didn't want to move. "Sally!" Her voice sharp as a needle got me up. I pulled on my clothes under the covers and, shivering, ran for the warmth of the fire. From afar, I heard the dull, regular thwack of Pa's ax.

"Your pa and Abe been in the woods since first light, cutting logs," Mama said. "They'll be back hungry as bears." She was wrapped in a blanket, covering her head and shoulders and tied around her middle with a cord. She handed me the pail to fetch water. "And don't lollygag around."

The spring was covered with a skim of ice. The water sparkled as it broke through and splashed out over the rocks. A flock of chickadees in the brush chattered at me. "Hello, hello," I said. I pulled some shriveled flower heads and held them out in my hand. One brave little soul flew down and pecked at the seeds, then flew off. I waited with my hand outstretched to see if another one would be as bold. Sure enough, another came, and another, and then there were two together on my hand. And then three! Maybe we didn't have folks nearby, but we had the birds for company.

Mama was waiting and I was hungry, but I didn't move. The birds were all around me, all over me, chattering in their busy little voices. Even after they flew off, even as I dipped my hands into the spring, gasping at the cold, and splashed water on my face, even as I carried the water down and set the pail near the fire, their voices were in my head.

The water was for the corn and oats Mama had pounded. Pa had shot a wild pig the day before, and a thick slab of bacon was sizzling on the fire. "Bring the drippings," Mama said. "Put them in the mash. Careful!" The mash smelled fearsome good, but there was no eating until Pa and Abe returned. Soon as I heard Abe whistling, I called out to Mama, "Here they come."

We all sat down by the fire, the trencher loaded with

the mash and the squabs Abe had shot, with the bacon on a log in the middle. Pa used the spoon first, then Abe, then me, and last, Ma. For a while, the only sounds were us chewing and biting and bones cracking.

Pa licked his fingers and said, "I've got a dozen logs cut, good, true, straight logs. A dozen more, Mrs. Lincoln, and I'm almost ready to raise your house."

"The Lord will provide," Mama said.

"He's provided enough snow," Pa said. "Me and the boy will be cutting soon. You'd be in your cabin right now, Mrs. Lincoln, if I had ten more boys good as Abe."

I looked over at my little brother. His face was all lighted up with Pa's praise. He was by the fire, wolfing down a chunk of johnnycake, his hair peppered with woodchips. Made me smile to see him like that, and Mama was smiling too. Pa praising Abe spread ease over us all.

Now that Pa was on his own land, there was more contentment in him. "A lot to do," he kept saying, "a man's got to keep working." But the feeling was good. When he pointed to the trees he was going to girdle, so we could plant in the spring, his face lit up just like Abe's was doing.

Pa was always talking about trees, the trees he'd cleared and the trees waiting to be cut, and the cedar and the poplar, and the ash and the chestnut he wanted for the cabin. "I only wish I'd dropped more trees when I was here in the fall," he said. He spit on the ax head and started sharpening it with a stone. "I should have done more then."

"No use burdening yourself with those thoughts," Mama said. "Best live in contentment, Mr. Lincoln. You did what you could, and that's as much as any man can do."

I knew Mama was right, God would provide, everything in its season, yet I leaned to Pa's way, wanting the cabin up and the trees pushed back and the trace widened, wanting a real road filled with wagons and people. Wanting! Wanting everything faster, sooner. Mama's way was acceptance and contentment. I wanted to be more like her, too, but how hard it was!

Later that day, Mama and I worked at weaving evergreen branches into the sides of our shelter and over the top to make it warmer. I heard a bell tinkling a long way off. The snow had finally stopped and the air was icy clear. "Mama! Somebody's coming." She stopped and listened. "Do you hear it, Mama? We're going to have a visitor."

No sooner I said it, than he appeared, a big knobby-kneed boy coming through the trees, sitting on the back of an ox. "Here you is!" he said, as if he'd produced us himself. "I told Pa I heard folks! I said, 'I hear them,' and here you is. I'm Tyler and my pa is Fletcher and my ma is Rachel. Ma says to tell you we're the Littles from back home in Kentucky. You recollect us?"

"I do," I said. "We were in school together, and you couldn't hold still or keep your mouth shut. You got birched more than most, Tyler Little."

"Sally," Mama said. "Your mouth! No need to discomfort the boy."

"It's the plain truth, Mrs. Lincoln," Tyler said, "plain as this nose on my face. That schoolmaster took the birch to me more times than you could count. Now I'm through with school! Didn't never learn nothing useful there anyway."

"Well, we're pleased to see you, Tyler," Mama said, "and you tell your mama it's a comfort to know you're all so near."

"We been here better'n a year now, Mrs. Lincoln. When your mister come to mark your land, he and my pa walked the boundaries together. Glad you're here safe and sound," he finished, and he rode off, the bell jingling.

The next day, the whole Little family came on a sled pulled through the woods by a pair of oxen. Mr. Little was a queer-looking man, one side of his face pulled down, the other side pulled up. He didn't talk much, just looked all around.

I was afraid he'd catch me staring at him. I knew I shouldn't be doing that, but I couldn't hardly stop myself. I was glad when he went off with Pa and the boys to look at the logs for the cabin, and I could pay attention to Mama and Mrs. Little, who wasn't little at all. She was taller than Mama and lots bigger around, and she more than made up for Mr. Little's silence in talk and friendliness.

She'd brought Mama a pot of soup and a loaf of wheat bread baked fresh that morning.

"That bread's real welcome, Mrs. Little," I said.

"Thankee, Sally. That's a fine girl you've got there, Mrs. Lincoln. I been looking out for you folks for days now, praying hard that your journey was a safe one. I knowed you was coming, but we never seen no smoke. But then my boy Tyler said he heard something. I listened hard as I could, but I didn't hear nothing, but Tyler—he's like a hound after a rabbit—he insisted, so his father finally let him loose."

All the time she was talking, she was looking around at our camp, at the open-faced shelter and the fire pit. "Mmm, mmm," she said. "I could never live primitive like this. I want four walls around me and a roof overhead. That's what I told Mr. Little when he said we was moving to Indiana territory. I said, 'Mr. Little, you won't see me till you have a cabin built I can step into.'"

"Mama," I said, before I could stop myself, "that's what you should have told Pa."

"Sally," Mama said. "Will you never keep a lock on that tongue of yours?"

Mrs. Little patted my shoulder. "Well, Mrs. Lincoln, you and your young 'uns can come and stay with us till your cabin's finished. It would be real welcome to me to have company."

"Isn't that the kindest thing you ever heard, Mama," I cried.

"Thankee, Mrs. Little," Mama said. "I'll talk to Mr. Lincoln on the subject."

Later, when she told Pa of Mrs. Little's neighborly offer, I didn't say a word, but I was listening hard and making up Pa's answer. *Yes, much obliged, Mrs. Little. Thankee for a fine offer. We'll be coming right along.*

"Got too much to do to be trekking back and forth," Pa said. "It ain't so bad here, is it, Mrs. Lincoln? We're under cover, and there's a good fire and plenty of wood to feed it."

"That's right," Mama said.

I knew she would. She always agreed with Pa! I tried to be like her, tried and tried, but there was a goodness and patience in Mama that I could never find in me.

After the Littles' visit, other neighbors stopped by, some old friends from back home, some we were just meeting, and Mama's relatives, too, the Hankses, who lived seven miles away, all of them ready to help Pa raise our cabin. It was a glad time, and I didn't feel near so alone as before.

═══ CHAPTER 10 ═══

Amanda, We're Just Resting

One morning, Pa looked up at the sky and we all looked up with him. Our patch of sky, all we could see, had been growing as the trees came down, and this morning it was scrubbed white. "I'm hitching up Branch," Pa said, "and Abe and me are going to start snaking logs out of the woods."

"I'm feared you're working that boy too hard, Mr. Lincoln," Mama said. Abe was sitting next to her.

"Sally," Pa said, just like Mama hadn't even spoke, "I want you to follow the Indian Trace, get over to the neighbors, and pass on the message that Tom Lincoln is ready to commence raising his house and would be glad for any help."

"Mr. Lincoln," Mama said, "it's a good piece for the girl to go alone. Send Abe with her."

"No, I'm not going to do that. I need him. The trail is marked, Mrs. Lincoln. I seen to that myself, left slash marks all the way to Parrot Creek. It's only two miles to where the track crosses the creek and another three to the Littles. She'll have the dogs with her and no trouble if she don't dawdle. Sal, I expect you'll be back before dark."

"Yes, Pa," I said. I wasn't keen to be off alone, but proud that Pa had asked me. Before I left, Mama combed my hair and braided it in one long hank and tied it off with a ribbon. She put a chunk of corn bread in a sack, and I tied it around my waist and set Amanda alongside.

The trail was bare in spots, the snow uneven, drifted high in some places and thin and crusty in others. For a while the dogs kept right with me, the little one that Abe and I had named Samson hardly breaking the crust, and the big one, Goliath, crashing through everything. They were good company, but as soon as they got wind of squirrel or bird in the thickets, they'd disappear.

I swung along, eyeing the trees ahead for Pa's slash marks and cutting left and right to avoid branches fallen across the path. The trees gleamed and swayed over me. I was keeping a good pace, then I come on a tree blocking my way, too big to even climb over. I broke from the path to go around it, and a grouse exploded out from under the snow and flew up in my face. "Scared me," I yelled and jumped aside. When I looked around again, I was lost. I didn't know where I was. The track had disappeared.

I moved on ahead, sure that I'd come on the track in a few steps. Seemed as if I just got deeper into the trees. I turned one way and then the other. Nothing but trees in every direction. No track, no slash marks, and no sky to help me find my way.

I sat down on a log to think and ordered my noisy heart to still down. The woods were full of rustles and thumps and creaks. I ate the corn bread Mama had given me. "We're not lost," I told Amanda, "and I ain't afeared, just resting. You're resting too."

I know that. We don't get lost.

"Where do you think those dang dogs are?"

Oh, they'll show up. You know what Pa says. Dogs always know where they are.

Around us, the forest stirred with the chittering of squirrels and the windy crowds of birds. Beneath me, the earth breathed, heavy and dank, a hidden world of unseen creatures, insects and spiders, grubs and worms and moles.

"Amanda, remember what Mama says?"

Of course I do! If you lose your way, stay still. Call out.

"I wouldn't question Mama. You know that, Amanda. But who would hear me now if I called out?"

The dogs, Sally. They'll hear you.

I squeezed Amanda and climbed up on the log and shouted as loud as I could, "Samson! Goliath!" I listened. Nothing but birds and my voice swallowed up in the tangle.

"Samson! Goliath!" I shouted and shouted their names. Amanda told me to keep yelling, so I did. And a few minutes later, as if guided by a divine hand, Goliath came crashing through the undergrowth. He was panting and—I knew Pa would say it was my fancy—but he was smiling.

He ran, I followed him, and he brought me straightaway to the trace, first to Pa's blaze, then to the creek with its log bridge and the path on the other side. The creek was a wondrous place! It shimmered yellow and green with ducks and pigeons and parakeets, hundreds of them, thousands of them, maybe millions, all of them noisily rising into the air, then dropping back into the water. Pa said if you knew where they roosted, you didn't even need a gun. You could knock them off the trees by the dozens with a stick. I started looking around for a stick or a branch, then I remembered my mission. There was no time

The log that bridged the creek was wet and slick. I stepped out on it and right away my foot slipped. I caught myself and stopped, looking down at the icy rocks and the water foaming over them.

"Are you all right, Amanda?"

Yes, Sally. Keep going.

A deep breath, and I started across again, my arms out for balance, putting down one foot, then the other.

I was almost over to the other side when Goliath suddenly ran into the water, scaring up a roaring raft of ducks. They rose up beneath me and around me, and I lost my balance again and almost went into the creek. I threw myself forward and landed on the bank with my face in the snow. "Goliath," I yelled, as he came splashing up the bank, "look what you made me do." He panted and smiled and shook himself so that water flew every which way.

I ran the rest of the way to the Littles, and Goliath ran with me. At the Littles', first thing, I went inside and delivered my message to Mr. Little. He squinted at me with his twisted face and said, "Tell your pa I'll spread the word."

"Sally," Mrs. Little said, "set a bit and warm up." She had me sit by the fire to dry off, then fed me a steaming bowl of pudding. "I only wish I had a girl child like you," she said. "But all the Lord gave me was my boy. It's a pleasure to me to have you sitting by my fire." Mrs. Little made much of me, wanted me to stay and eat with them, stay the night and go back the next day.

"I sure would like to," I said. After a month living

outdoors and in the half shelter, it was strange and wonderful to be able to stand up and have four walls around me. "But my pa is going to be looking for me, and my mama needs me," I said.

To my surprise, Mr. Little insisted on walking back to the creek with me. He took his rifle and said he was going to get some birds. He never said another word the whole way, but Tyler was with us, and he was as good company as his mama. Their dogs, three of them, came along with my two. Samson had showed up, covered in mud.

When we got to the creek, it was coming on dusk, and the birds were coming down to roost. They came screaming through the trees, a cloud of yellow and green packing into every twig and limb. Mr. Little raised his gun and shot twice. Tyler ran around, knocking birds off the branches. They were all over the ground, adults and squabs. They fell everywhere. Some, with broken wings, were floundering toward the water. Tyler and I started snatching them up and snapping their necks. "Sally, these are the best eating birds." He licked his lips. "Them and the ducks."

We kept the squabs and threw the rest to the dogs. When we were done, Mr. Little's bag bulged. He tied together a bunch of birds and gave them to me to bring home. With him and Tyler watching, I went across the bridge without slipping once. Then I went on, saying to myself what I would tell Mama and Pa and Abe about the day's doings.

CHAPTER 11

Dreaming About Our Cabin

The day of the house raising, we were all up before dawn. Pa hitched up Branch, and he and Abe dragged the logs into the clearing where our cabin was going to rise. I was jumping with excitement, thinking about having a real place to live in again. How I wished I could be doing that work with Pa and Abe, but I had to keep with Mama, neatening around our camp and feeding the fire to get it going high. Mama had had a meat stew simmering all night, preparing for the people coming to help us.

"Snow on the ground," she said, "but it's a beautiful clear day, Sally. The Lord provides. A good day for a house raising."

The Littles were the first to arrive, Tyler with a big hello for me and Abe. Mr. Little had a nod for Mama and raised a hand in salute to Pa. Then that silent man said to me, "How's this fine young woman doing?"

Didn't my feathers flare! "Just fine, thankee, Mr. Little," I said. "I'm helping out my mama."

"The way it should be," he said, and the half of his face that were pulled up, pulled up some more. It was a smile!

Mrs. Little called me over to their wagon, gave me a real nice greeting, and then the two of us unloaded a stack of long boards to make tables. "We knew you'd have plenty of spare stumps to set them on," she said with a big laugh.

We set up three tables, and we could have used more. Beginning with the Littles, every family brought food. They kept coming from farms for miles around. Soon as the women got down from their wagons, they'd give a howdy to Mama and me, and then they'd carry their bowls and pots of food over to the tables and set them down.

The men were standing around with their mauls and saws and axes, talking about the weather. "Smoke's rising good," Pa said.

"Yup, that's clear weather," another man said.

Then a third chimed in, "I seen a heavy mist in the hollows. Sun'll burn it off. No snow today."

The tables filled with trenchers of roast turkeys, a saddle of deer meat, squash and potato pies, roasted turnips and beans, bowls of wild honey, a peck of apples and another of pawpaws. Besides whiskey for the men and toddies for the ladies, there was a dizzying lot of teas, mint and wild strawberry, sage, catnip, sassafras, and blackberry root tea. I'd never seen so much food and all of it smelling powerful good.

Mama and me and a few of the other women carried around the food, offering it, and stepping between the young 'uns playing tag and chasing each other. The men put down their tools and started in eating. Folks were sitting on stumps and leaning against trees, eating as fast as they could and talking as if they hadn't had a chance, ever, to speak their minds. I was real curious to hear what everyone was saying, but I was lucky to hear anything, what with the clattering of pots and the horses neighing and the dogs yipping and the children screaming and calling.

Some of the men were talking about a man named Daniel Turner who never showed up for house raisings. "You ain't gonna get blood out of a turnip," Mr. Little said, and another man drawled, "Son-of-a-gun's too lazy to scare the flies out of his mouth." At that, the other men slapped the table so hard it almost went over.

Listening to them livened me up so, I was almost sorry when they got up to go to work.

"Fellers," Pa said, "I got trees that are two foot through, and I sawed them in twenty- and ten-foot lengths."

The men nodded approvingly. "That'll be a good-sized cabin," Mr. Little said. "Plenty of room for you all."

It was but a step from the tables to where our cabin was going to rise. Pa had marked out the corners, and the men all set to, bringing in the logs and putting them in place. Pa asked Mr. Little to be the south-corner man. Mr. Adams, Mr. Smith, and Mr. Wayland each took another corner, and each of them notched his end of the log before it was set in place. Then Pa checked that the logs were straight and level.

I had to stay with Mama and the other ladies to help prepare for the next meal, but every chance I got, I ran to watch the men. Log on top of log was going up on all four sides. It was a wonder to see how quick walls were rising up from the ground!

Abe and Tyler and some of the other boys were chipping away at the logs. "Look here, Sally," Tyler said, showing off how he used the broad ax. "See how I'm shaving slivers of wood from one side and then the other. See how smooth and slick they are."

"Let me try." I reached for the ax. It had a short handle

and a heavy head. It was hard to control, and my first swings were wild, but I got better. I was shaving off those slivers, but Tyler couldn't stop correcting me.

"The slivers have to be smooth," he said.

"I know. You told me that."

"The trick is not to dig too deep."

"I'm not digging too deep, Tyler."

"Careful there! You don't want to bash your leg."

"I won't!" He got me so frazzled, I swung the ax and hit the side of my leg. It weren't a cut, but it hurt, and I let out a howl.

"Not that easy, is it?" Tyler said. "I had to learn."

"I did as good as you, Tyler."

"Maybe even better," Abe said.

"Thankee, Abe!" I wanted to prove it, but Mama was calling me that she needed water, and I never did get to claim that ax again.

By midday, the walls were raised six logs high all around. The grunting and hollering of the men and the clamor of mauls and saws died down. Everyone was ready to eat again. Me too, but the men first. I kept glancing over at our roofless cabin. I wanted them to eat and get back to work.

I kept dreaming about our cabin. It would have a roof. And we'd have a corncrib for the corn we'd plant in the spring, and a roost for the hens Mama would get, and a pen for pigs, and maybe even a fenced place for our own cow.

That afternoon, there were no more side walls to raise, but at both ends the walls kept rising, narrowing to the peak. We were all watching as Pa and three other men raised one side of the roof beam and then the other. We lifted our voices in a mighty cheer when the roof beam was set in place. I think my voice was louder than anyone else's.

By the time the roof was fairly covered with sheets of bark, it was late, and the sun was sinking into the trees. Fires were lit in the cleared area near the tables, and Pa called everyone down. "Time to celebrate! The work is done for you fellers."

One of the men stood up in the clearing, crossed his arms, and started reciting and then singing, "Should old acquaintance be forgot and never brought to mind?"

Other people joined in, "Should old acquaintance be forgot in days of auld lang syne?"

The women were setting out food again and talking among themselves. Some of the girls were off making a snowman, and Mama told me to join them, but I lingered. I liked listening to the female talk! One of the ladies, named Mrs. Mary King, who was near as tall as Mama, but bigger around, was telling about her man.

"Mr. King told me he didn't want to hear my mouth moving 'less he asked me to speak. His lordship don't like being disturbed. He expects me to be setting in the corner by the fireplace, finger in my mouth, looking out the sides of my eyes, waiting for him to speak to me."

I looked over at Mama. She was smiling. "Did you rattle Mr. King's ears?" she said.

"I did. But I should have sewed up his pockets, too."

Another lady said, "I'd of peppered his tea and spit in his soup." They were all laughing.

When the men crowded around the table, I looked for Mr. King and got another surprise. He was a little man with a big voice. I was glad he wasn't my pa.

When everyone was settled down, eating, I slipped into the cabin through the door opening. Pa would have to make us a regular door shutter and a floor and a fireplace, but the cabin was raised and I was standing in it! It was dark inside, but there were walls around me and a roof over my head. I touched the walls all the way around, then stood by the door opening and looked out.

The boys had started wrestling, and the men were cheering them on. Abe and Tyler grasped each other's belts. Abe was as tall as Tyler and a lot skinnier, but he was strong. They kept trying to throw each other to the ground without letting go of the belt. It was all rough and tumble. Abe went down first, and then they faced off again. Abe did well, but Tyler won. I ran out and hugged my brother. Then he went right off to tell Mama how he did, and I went over to join the girls, who were dancing.

The merriment went on for hours. The little ones were put to sleep in the wagons, and I was ready to sleep myself, but I didn't want to miss out on anything. I kept up for a good long time. When the last wagon left, I crept under the quilt in our half shelter next to Abe, who was already there, sound asleep.

CHAPTER 12

Ain't Never Enough Time

Spring came, and Mama and I were out every day picking the early greens—ramps, dandelions, and plantains. The flies and bugs were something terrible. Abe and I never left off scratching the bites on our arms and necks. We scratched ourselves bloody. In the field, Pa had brush piles smoldering day and night, and that helped some.

Mama got irritated with us. "Now that we have a cabin, we should be thankful and not be mentioning bugs all the time. Every time you strike a bug, I want you to say, 'bless you.'"

"Bless you," Abe yelled, smacking his arm. "Now you say it, Sally."

I gave him an evil eye and smacked my head where the bugs were bothering me. Truth was, I *was* thankful and grateful to God, that the bears and panthers were outside and we were inside, and I was thankful that Pa had his rifle nearby, but the bugs didn't care about inside or outside, and I was never going to bless any of them!

Our cabin was spacious, but there was the four of us, and the dogs when they could get in, and Mama's wheel in the corner, and our things still in sacks. Pa had promised Mama that once we had a cabin, he'd give her pegs and build her a corner cabinet and plenty of shelves, but he never had the time. Pa never had the time to do anything in the cabin, 'less Mama begged him to do it. We were all sleeping on the floor till Mama begged a bed out of Pa. Our table was still a couple of boards on stumps, and the walls never got chinked proper, neither, so there was always something blowing in, wind or dust. Most days Mama kept herself wrapped tight in her shawl.

It was Mama and me who wedged pegs between the logs so we could hang clothes, and Mama and me who carried buckets of sand up from the creek to cover the dirt floor. Mama showed me how to broom the sand smooth. That was my job every day, and I liked doing it, making swirls and circles in the sand with the broom. It was real pretty till somebody stepped on it.

Abe noticed my designs and went tiptoe around the cabin, but Pa never noticed anything, just clumped through. But like Mama said, he was tuckered from working in the fields all day. When he came in, it was just to eat and go out again. As long as there was light, Pa was working. Some of the giant trees he couldn't ax no way, but he girdled them, so the leaves wouldn't come and take away the light. When he plowed, he wound in and out around the stumps, with Abe following, dropping the seeds.

One day, Mr. King, who was a stonemason and, Pa said, made the straightest walls in the county, came by to help Pa make a stone fireplace. He and Pa had been bartering since the house raising. Pa had built Mr. King a horse barn, then helped him buy a horse. Pa knew everything about horses. We got a cow in return. That was some nice day when Pa came home leading the cow and carrying her newborn calf in his arms!

And now we were getting us a stone fireplace. Pa and Mr. King didn't have time to build the chimney, though. "Come spring, there ain't never enough time for everything," Mr. King said, at the end of the day. "We'll get to it by and by."

Mama and I were so excited that we could cook inside now and keep a fire on cold nights, but it weren't no good. Without the chimney, every gust of wind sent smoke and soot into the cabin. Mama and me were coughing and rubbing our stinging eyes all day, and at night, Abe's eyes teared so bad he stopped even trying to read. That sure made him morose.

"I never seen a boy with such a long face," Pa said. He started in coughing, got up, and spit out a gob of mucus through the door opening.

"We need a chimney, Pa," I said.

"I know that, Sally! I'm going to throw up a mud and stick chimney and be done with it."

Well, he said it, but he didn't get to it, and Mama finally had enough. In the morning, after Pa and Abe went out to the fields, Mama and me went out and cut armfuls of pin-cherry twigs and laid them down in the cabin. Next we brought buckets of clay up from the riverbank. "Never done this before," Mama said, "but I believe the two of us can figure it out, Sally."

We did, too! We made us a mud and stick chimney, and we were proud. We got our fire going good and when we saw the smoke going up that chimney and out of the cabin, we clapped our hands. I couldn't hardly wait for Pa to see what Mama and me had done.

When he come in for chow, though, he stood in front of the fireplace, spraddle legged, looking up at our chimney and *laughing*. "That's the most pitiful-looking chimney I ever saw," he said. "Lopsided and crooked."

Mama's forehead wrinkled, but she didn't say nothing.

I did, though. "Pa, there ain't no smoke in the cabin," I said. "The chimney Mama and me made, it's working."

"Hmm, hmm," Pa said. He rocked back on his heels. "You got a true point there, Sally."

That night, Abe was reading again, and no one was coughing.

When we had a spell of rainy days, Pa built a sleeping platform for Abe and me. Carpentry sure was what Pa favored. He whistled all the while he was building the platform. He never whistled when he plowed. Then the rain stopped, and Pa said he didn't have time to make us a ladder for the platform.

Abe and me went into the woods and picked out a small straight tree. Abe axed it down and we dragged it back to the cabin. Mama wanted me to come inside and help get ready for dinner. "Give me five more minutes, Mama," I begged.

Abe trimmed the branches short for footholds. I tidied up after him. We were almost finished when Pa came back. I thought he'd be glad Abe had made the ladder, but he were in a temper. He gave Abe a thump and knocked him aside. "You ain't good for nothing," he said. "Git. I'll finish it myself."

Abe stomped off around the side of the cabin. I went after him. "Don't mind Pa," I said. "Don't mind him, Abe. He's just tuckered, like Mama says."

"I don't mind him." Abe picked up a clod of dirt and threw it. "He didn't have to strike me. Why'd he have to do that?"

"It's just the way he is," I said. "He don't mean nothing by it."

"I'd of finished the job."

"I know you would have," I said.

"Pa can't wait for nothing."

"I know," I said again. Why was Pa so mean to Abe?

Mama was calling to me to milk the cow. "Come with me, Abe," I said. I got the milking pail, and Abe and I went out to the fence where the calf was tethered. "Ho, Bessie, Bessie, Bessie, ho," we called, and the cow came plodding up to us. She'd been foraging along the creek.

"Good girl." I brought the calf to her and let her suck.

"Someday," Abe said, "when I grow up and can do what I want—"

"Can't till you're twenty-one," I said.

"—know what I'm going to do, Sal?" he went on. "I'm going to go away. I'm not staying here! No, sir. I'm going to go away and never come back."

"Not even to see me?" I said.

"Well . . . maybe I'll come back to see you. And Mama, too."

"That's good," I said. "I'd sure miss you, if I never saw you again."

"Milk's flowing good," hc said, pointing to Bessie.

I pulled the calf away and milked Bessie, filling the bucket. Then I took a drink for myself, and Abe did too.

CHAPTER 13

We Get Lightning

*M*ama and me were outside, pegging clothes on the line, when a man came by, leading a big white mare with a sagging back. "I'm Enoch Smith here, come to talk to your mister," he said to Mama. He spit on the ground. "I hear your man knows horses. I come to do some trading."

Mama sent Abe to fetch Pa out of the field. She invited Mr. Smith to come in, set, and have a cup of coffee and a biscuit. "Neighborly of you, Mrs. Lincoln," he said. He had that biscuit gone almost before Mama set it down before him. After that, he gulped down the coffee, then got up and spit in the fire. I saw on Mama's face that she didn't like that one bit, but she didn't say nothing.

When Pa came in, he took off his hat and shook hands with Mr. Smith. We all clustered around the table to listen to what he had to say to Pa. "Mr. Lincoln," he started, "I hear you been raising pigs."

Pa nodded. "You hear correct."

"I need me a porker," Mr. Smith said. "You got one for me?"

Pa tapped his fingers on the table, then he looked at me and said, "Sal, you reckon we got a extra porker for Mr. Enoch Smith?" Pa said it as if he didn't know the answer. "You reckon we can spare one of our porkers?"

"Yes, Pa, I believe we can," I said, real polite, and Mama nodded her head approvingly.

"My girl says we got a porker for you," Pa said. "What you got for us?"

"I'll trade you my mare out there. I love her dearly. Her name is Elsie," he said. "She's a fine horse. It's going to hurt me to let her go."

"Well, let me take another look at her," Pa said. We all trailed him outside. Elsie's eyes were big and kind. I petted her nose. Pa opened her mouth to look at her teeth, lifted her legs, and ran his hand over her sway back.

Elsie twitched her nose at me, and I knew we had to have her.

"This horse is lame," Pa said, shaking his head. "She's

as old as Methuselah, Mr. Smith. Why would I be wanting an old lame, slow mare?"

"But, Pa," I burst out. "She's so nice. Look at her, Pa, she's sweet!"

"Sal, keep that mouth of yours shut," Pa said, fixing his eye on me.

"Sorry, Pa," I muttered. Mama pulled me close to her.

"This horse ain't good for much," Pa said. "She's got ulcers on her leg too. She can hardly stand. Poor old girl." He walked all around Elsie again. "Anybody that takes this horse will be doing you a big favor, Mr. Smith."

"She's strong as a mule," Mr. Smith said. He switched around the wad of tobacco in his mouth and spit. "It would be more'n a fair trade, Mr. Lincoln. One porker for this fine mare. What do you say?"

Pa sighed deeply. He appeared to be thinking. "Abe," he said, finally. "Guess we ought to do the neighborly thing. Fetch one of the young porkers from the pen."

Abe came running back, holding an armful of squealing pig. "That's what you want to trade?" Mr. Smith said. "Must be this is the runt of the litter."

"He's a sturdy fellow," Pa said. "I guarantee he'll fatten right up."

"Well, I'll do you a favor and take it." Mr. Smith tied

a rope around the porker's neck, grumbling all the while that it was a weakling, small fellow. Then he and Pa shook hands, he spit one more time, and he left.

It didn't take Pa but a week or so to heal the mare's leg, so she was over being lame, but she never did get over being slow. I was the one loved Elsie the most, the way she looked at me, it was as if she knew everything I was thinking. I liked her name, too, but Abe said, "She's so slow, we got to give her a name for that. Like Lightning. That's the name for her!"

He was real taken with this idea, and he wouldn't call her nothing but Lightning. I fussed a bit, but I didn't really care. Elsie was just as nice when she was Lightning, and her eyes were just as big and brown and sweet.

CHAPTER 14

Kinfolk Coming!

*O*ne afternoon we were all inside finishing the noon meal when we heard the letter carrier's horn. I was up from the table before Abe or anyone else. "Sally, come back here," Mama called. "Stop. I want you to walk."

I was wicked and pretended I didn't hear Mama. I ran outside, right up the path toward the letter carrier coming through the trees on his horse. I couldn't walk like a proper young lady when the letter carrier was coming to us!

"Good day to you!" I cried. "Are you looking for us? We're the Lincolns!" He didn't answer, just rode by me on his horse. He was a strong-looking fellow with yellow hair tied back. I would have admired him, if he wasn't so rude. Mama, Pa, and Abe were outside now. Mama put her hands on my shoulders and held me still.

"Good day, sir," the letter carrier said to Pa. "Are you Mr. Lincoln?"

"That's me, Tom Lincoln. Do you have a letter for me?" Pa held out his hand and the carrier leaned down and gave it to him.

If it'd been me, I'd have had that letter open in a second, but Pa didn't even look at it. He just held on to it. "Pa," I said, "who's it from? Won't you open it, Pa? Give it here, Pa, I'll read it to you."

Mama was eyeing the letter too, but she folded her hands over her stomach and said in her quiet voice, "A visitor is an occasion, Sally. Your Pa is going to jaw for a while."

Sure enough, Pa started right in with one of his stories, saying to the carrier, "Two days ago, I seen a bear along the trail up ahead. As big a one as I ever seen."

"Don't say," the carrier said.

"Must have stood sixteen hands, bigger than that horse you're riding."

"Don't say!"

"Yup," Pa said. "Weighed near half a ton. I couldn't see the path behind him for all his bulk. He was standing right up on his hind legs too, like he was one of us."

The carrier patted the gun slung alongside him. "What did you do, Mr. Lincoln? Did you take care of the feller?"

"Well, I'll tell you. Me without my gun, I had a mind to turn away, but Mr. Bear was sniffing at me, came right up close, so there was nothin' for it but to talk him out of making me his meal. I talked to him the way the Indians do, respectful like. 'Bear,' I said, and his ears perked right up. He was listening." Pa rocked back on his heels. 'Bear,' I said, 'I mean you no harm, and I don't want nothing from you.'"

"Well, sir," the carrier said, "you saying you and the bear was having a chew, just like you and me are, right now?"

"That's right," Pa said.

I looked over at Abe. He was grinning, ear to ear. He sure liked it when Pa started spinning a story.

"'I'm not much of a meal neither,' I told him," Pa kept going, "'all bony and tough as I am. I can tell you're a fine brave bear. All I want you to do is stand aside and let me pass, so I can do my work.' He was listening, those little black eyes watching me, and he seemed to like what I was saying. I don't know how long we was that way, before I bowed to him."

"First you *talked* to him and then you *bowed* to him?" the carrier man said.

"That's right," Pa said. "To show respect, and he was genuinely attentive."

Pa didn't crack a smile until the courier went on his way. Then he slapped his knee and guffawed. "You liked that, didn't you?" he said to Abe, and he gave him a tap on the head. Telling a whopper put Pa in a real good mood.

"Mr. Lincoln, the letter," Ma said.

"All right, Mrs. Lincoln." Pa examined the envelope front and back. Sniffed it too. Then he handed it over to Mama. She slit the envelope open and took out the sheet of paper.

"It's from my aunt Betsy Sparrow back in Kentucky," Mama said.

"Let me read it out to you, Mama," I begged.

"Patience, Sally."

Patience, patience. Why did I always have to have patience? Couldn't I just sometimes have impatience?

Mama started in slowly reading the letter out loud. "Dear Niece . . . your uncle . . . Mr. Thomas Sparrow and I . . . will be coming on to Indiana. . . ."

The way Mama was reading she would never get to the end! My hands craved to take the letter from her, and might be she caught on my thought, because she stopped reading and gave it to me.

Standing straight as I could and holding the letter in front of me with both hands, I read it out from the beginning.

Dear Niece, your uncle Mr. Thomas Sparrow and I will be coming on to Indiana to join you and Mr. Lincoln and your children very soon. We are aiming to leave from here before the end of the summer. We will be coming by horse and bringing our cow and her calf and also our nephew Dennis Hanks to accompany us. We are all in good health and spirits and hope you are the same.

I read good and loud, and never stumbled over a single word, although I knew I shouldn't think that. That was pride, and pride cometh before a fall. But it was true, I was a good reader.

When I finished, Mama took the letter and folded it and put it back in the envelope. "Now that is good news," she said. "My kinfolk are coming. I'm very partial to Aunt Betsy."

"Never did like that Tom Sparrow," Pa said.

"Why not, Pa?" I asked.

That got me a frown and a slap. "Mind your mouth, Sally. That's grown-up business."

Later, I told Abe, "I'm going to be the first to see Uncle Tom Sparrow and Aunt Betsy Sparrow arrive."

"No, you ain't. I'll see them first."

"No, you won't, Abraham Lincoln!"

"Yes, I will, Sarah Lincoln!"

"You won't."

"I will."

"You won't!"

We would of kept that up all day if Mama didn't stop us and send us off to do our chores.

Every day after that, I kept a sharp eye out for Mama's kinfolk. "When are they coming?" I pestered Mama. "I wish they'd hurry."

"Sally, a watched pot never boils. Do your chores and don't think about it so much."

I wasn't the only one hungry for the company, though. Ten times more, Mama had me or Abe read Aunt Betsy's letter out loud, and then she'd go to speculating on how long it would take them to make the journey and when they'd get here. "Got to be soon," she said. "Winter's in the air."

The leaves on the trees were all yellowing, and Mama had bunches of stuff, potherbs and teas, drying by the fire. She had me and Abe off gathering acorns and nuts too and picking the few pawpaws that remained. And the nights were turning real cool. Every time I got into bed, I had to hustle my feet up and down, up and down, to warm them up. Then I'd curl myself up like a possum, and Abe and me would trade talk and venture guesses about what Aunt Betsy Sparrow would bring with her. "Maybe some pretties for me," I said, "and a book for you."

With all our looking and waiting and waiting, I got to thinking they'd never come! And then one day, there they were, clattering into the yard with horses and a wagon, a cow and her calf, and all their goods. Aunt Betsy and Mama got their arms around each other, hugging and kissing so hard and joyful that Aunt Betsy's bonnet went sailing right off her head.

Cousin Dennis hung back. He was a tall one, older than me, and already had him a little mustache. "You a good worker?" Pa said, looking him over. Cousin Dennis nodded, sort of bashful.

I picked up Aunt Betsy's bonnet and brought it to her. "Thankee, Sally." She tied it on again, then took me by the hand and said, "You remember me, sweets?"

"Yes." I laughed. "You taught me my letters."

"That's right. You weren't but three years old and no bigger than a tadpole. And look at you now."

I twirled around for her. "I'm almost eleven. Near grown," I said.

"So you are. And Abe! I just can't believe how long and tall Abe has got. Look at this boy, Mr. Sparrow," she said. "Sprouted up like Jack's bean stalk! Did you ever see anything like it? Near as tall as his father, and him only eight years."

Uncle Sparrow had sat down on a tree stump. "That was some terrible journey we had us. Didn't think I'd live through it," he said to Mama. He was a bent-over, old-looking man, and peculiar looking, too, because the tip of his nose was gone.

"You think somebody bit it off?" I whispered to Abe.

"Could be," he whispered back. "Pa says when men go at each other, they're like fighting cocks. They tear off ears and fingers and try to gouge out the other feller's eyes."

I shuddered, but when I looked at Uncle Sparrow, I couldn't imagine him fighting *anyone*.

"Let's show your aunt Betsy and uncle Sparrow where they are going to sleep," Mama said. Abe led the way to the half camp, the open-faced shelter where we all had spent so many weeks before our cabin went up. "Now, Aunt Betsy," Mama said, "you know this is just temporary till you get your own place. Sally and I went over every bit of the roof, making sure it was dry."

"Then we spread sand on the floor," I said, "and heaps of those good-smelling spruce branches. That's where you put down your mattress, Aunt Betsy. You'll be cozy and warm as can be! We were."

"My, my," Aunt Betsy said. "Isn't this fine. All that

work!" She patted me on the head again. She was full of praise for Mama and me for fixing up the half camp. "Isn't this just fine, Mr. Sparrow?" she said.

Uncle Sparrow grunted. "How we going to get all our stash in here, tell me that."

"Oh, you must be tired," Aunt Betsy soothed. She bustled around, found their mattress in the wagon, and spread it out.

Uncle Sparrow lay right down. "Cover me up, Mrs. Sparrow. I ain't had a decent sleep since we left Kentucky." He raised up on one elbow and pointed at me. "Bring me some water, girl." I went and got a pail of water and a gourd and set them down near him. "Here," he said, not moving, "give me just a sip now." I had to dip the gourd and hold it right to his lips for him to drink.

From day one, Aunt Betsy pitched in with helping Mama, and Cousin Dennis did the same with Pa. Only Uncle Sparrow was content to sit by the fire and talk about his ailments and why he didn't have any strength and had to sleep more than anyone else. He could eat, though, and always snatched the biggest chunk of meat off the table. But if Pa looked for help, Uncle Sparrow's knees were acting up, his back ached something fierce, his stomach was sour, and his throat was mean sore.

"That man's got more excuses for why he can't work

than a dog has fleas," Pa said to Mama. "Pure and simple, he's hog-in-the-mud lazy."

I wasn't supposed to hear that, but I was glad I did. Uncle Sparrow had me running and fetching like I was his personal servant. He was all the time sending me to fetch him a little extra food or another blanket. He was too tired to milk their cow or bring her in from the pasture. "But you'll do it for your old uncle, won't you, Sal," he'd say.

And I would. And I did. Like Mama said, Uncle Sparrow was our guest, and we had to treat him right. When he and Aunt left us a few weeks later to go on to a neighbor's where there was land and a house they could live in, I wasn't one bit sorry to see him leave, but Aunt Betsy and Cousin Dennis—that was different.

Cousin Dennis would fetch me anything I asked for and never a sour look. He and Abe had got to be like brothers too. Different as their ages were, they hit it off like dogs in dirt. Made me think Abe was longing deep down for a big brother.

"Dennis is a fine boy," Mama judged, "never forgot to bring something for the pot."

"He knows how to work," Pa said. "Think the Sparrows would trade Dennis for Abe?"

"Pa! I don't want to trade away Abe," I said.

"That's a joke, Sal. A funny. Ain't you got no sense of humor?"

"Oh," I said. "That was a joke. Oh." I looked over at my brother. He was hunched down by the fire, reading. If he heard Pa, you couldn't tell. He never even raised his head. He had his book open, but his eyes were squinched so tight shut I didn't think he could even see a word.

━── CHAPTER 15 ──━

Abe Never Switched No Animal!

*O*ne morning when I went for the cornmeal, I found the sack near empty. I'd noticed it the day before, but forgot to mention it to Mama. I stood there for a moment, being sorry that I was at fault and wishing there was some way I didn't have to tell Mama.

"Sal, what are you dreaming about?" she said. She was at her wheel.

"Mama." I tried to keep my voice regular. "No johnnycake today." I held up the empty sack.

"Now, how did that happen?" Mama said, like I knew she would.

"I forgot to tell you," I said.

"Oh, Sal! When are you going to grow up?"

"I'm trying," I said, looking down at my feet. "What are we going to make for breakfast for Pa?"

"There's more'n one way to skin a cat," Mama said, and she put me to work pounding corn into meal. By the time Pa and Abe came in from the fields to eat, we had johnnycake, like always.

When Pa was through eating, Mama told him we were out of cornmeal, and it was time to go to the mill. "I can do it," I said. I figured I ought to be the one to make up for my careless ways. Besides, riding my darling Lightning over to Butler's Mill would be a lot better than staying with Mama and scrubbing clothes. This was washing day.

"Going to the mill is a man's job," Abe said. "Those sacks are heavy. Pa always sends me. You don't even know the way."

"I do so," I said. "And I can lift a sack as good as you. Besides, I won't spend the whole day pranking around with the boys, like you do."

"Send me, Pa," Abe said. "You know I can do the job better than Sally."

"No, he can't, Pa! He's just boasting. Send me!"

"You two are the mouthiest young 'uns in the territory," Pa said. "This is Abe's job, Sal, and your job is right here with your mama."

That was that. No more arguing. In the middle of the afternoon, I was still scrubbing bedclothes when Tyler

Little came running, yelling out, even before he reached us, that Abe was killed.

"What's that boy saying?" Mama cried.

"Abe is killed at the mill, Mrs. Lincoln!" Tyler Little was panting. "He's killed, downright killed."

I grabbed Tyler Little by the face. "My brother ain't dead! You're a liar, Tyler Little." I squeezed his face so tight, his eyes bugged out.

Pa had come running in from the field. "What's all the noise about here? Sal, what you doing to that boy? Let go of him!"

Tyler took a big gulp of breath. "Your boy's lying on the ground, Mr. Lincoln. Abe! He ain't moving. It's that horse of his, kicked him in the head after he switched her."

"Abe never switched no animal," I said. I wanted to grab him again and hit him for saying such things. Abe had the biggest heart in the world for animals.

"Yes, he did. He switched that horse. I seen him. And that horse got mad and kicked Abe in the head and killed him dead."

Pa didn't say nothing more, just started running down the path toward the mill. By the time Mama and I started running, Pa was out of sight. None of us didn't even think to hitch up Branch. Butler's Mill wasn't that far, less than two miles off, but it seemed like those miles stretched forever, seemed like Mama and me were running and running and running and never getting there.

We were passing some new-fenced land when we saw Mr. Little's wagon coming toward us, with Mr. Little holding the reins. Pa was sitting up next to him with Abe in his arms, holding him just like Abe was dead. Mama and me ran to the wagon, both of us crying and wailing out Abe's name. "Hush, you women," Pa said.

And right then, like a miracle, Abe stirred, lifted his head up, and said, "Mama?"

"He's alive!" I cried out.

Mama knelt down, raised her eyes, and thanked the Lord. I walked alongside the wagon and reached up now and then to pat on Abe. I wanted to jump up there and hug him, but Pa was holding him tight.

Turned out Tyler Little was a false prophet—Abe was alive as any of us. Turned out *I* was wrong too. I should have known Abe weren't no saint! Lightning had been doing her work, pulling the millstone round, but she was too slow for Abe. He *did* use the switch on her, and she did kick him. And maybe I was wrong about Pa, too. I mean about his always being so hard on Abe. I seen the tender look on his face when he was holding Abe so close. It was a look I wouldn't never forget.

CHAPTER 16

Learning You a Lesson

*L*ightning's kick left a lump on Abe's head that we could all see. Mama put a plaster on it, but for a while he still had headaches and real strange dreams about birds that towered over people who were the size of insects and hid under leaves and in the cracks of trees. Abe fretted over those dreams. "I died," he told me one day. "I heard spirits talk, Sally."

"You didn't die," I said. I needed to correct him. "You were just asleep, and when you heard Mama's voice, you woke up. When you die, you don't come back, Abraham. You go to the Lord or you go to the Devil, and if you aren't good enough for the Lord or bad enough for the Devil, they got another place for you, where you stay till the Second Coming."

"The ways of the Lord are inscrutable," Abe said, leaping up on a stump. Pa had been away some days working for the Grigsbys, some of our close neighbors. They had a store and Pa had been engaged to put up shelves. With Pa gone, Abe still had work to do, but he was freer, jumping around more and funning with me.

"Could be I'm a ghost, Sally," he said. "Wooooo!" He waved his long skinny arms.

I grabbed him and pulled him down off the stump. "You shouldn't have switched Lightning."

"You told me that already, and I know it anyway."

"Horses have feelings just like you and me."

"She didn't have to kick me that hard."

"She was learning you a lesson, Abraham."

"Oh, a lesson! You sound like Pa, Sally."

We locked arms and wrestled and larked around until Mama called to us to stop being foolish and bring in wood.

Pa came home the next day from the Grigsbys' place. He had left with Branch loaded with his carpentry tools, but he came back with Branch hitched to a wagon. His tools were in back, along with a big white swan he'd shot on the way home.

"Where'd you get the wagon, Pa?" I asked.

"Mr. Grigsby traded it to me for my work."

Abe and I walked around and around, admiring it. It

was a small wagon, but big enough for all of us to ride on. Then Mama came out and looked the wagon over. "This will be real useful, Mr. Lincoln," she said.

Later, after Mama had plucked the bird and while she was making a stuffing of cornmeal and herbs, Pa told her about his trip.

"I seen your uncle Tom Sparrow while I was over there. He told me their cow has the trembles."

Mama looked up from stuffing the bird. "The trembles!"

Pa nodded. "I warned Tom Sparrow not to milk her. I told him not to touch that cow, to tie her up and not to even go near her."

"Did you say it forcefully, Mr. Lincoln?" Mama asked.

"I did, Mrs. Lincoln. And I told young Hanks, too, but they, none of them, didn't seem to think nothing of it. Cows have tremors sometimes, that's what they said. I told them, this ain't Kentucky. When cows get the trembles in this country, it's time to step lightly and get clear of that place."

"What are the trembles?" I asked. "What does that mean? Why do they have to tie up the cow?" Nobody answered.

"Your uncle Sparrow is fine, complaining like always, it's your aunt Betsy who's feeling poorly."

Mama's hand flew to her mouth. "How poorly?"

"Well, now, I don't know, but she's taken to her bed," Pa said.

Mama trussed the bird up on the stake. "Mind the fire, Sally," she said, and she and Pa went off in the corner to talk low. Later, Mama told me that cows with tremors could bring on the milk sickness to folks.

"Aunt Betsy'll be all right, won't she?" I said. "Don't she just need a little rest, like when you're feeling poorly?"

"Only the Lord knows," Mama said.

That night, I kept thinking on Aunt Betsy, how kind she was, and remembering how she had taught me my letters so long ago. Close by, Abe twisted and called out in his sleep. I wondered, were spirits talking to him again? I looked up into the buzzing darkness. What was roaming above us? Spirits, invisible beings, ghosts, and creatures who could harm us? The Devil could take any form. I prayed to God to make Aunt Betsy well, and I finally slept.

In the morning, when I came down the ladder, Mama was making up a pack of herbs and roots. "I'm going over to look in at Aunt Betsy," she said. "Pray the Lord it's only a fever. I'll make her some teas and a soup to spark her appetite, see what I can do for her. I'll be home in a day or two."

"Let me go with you," I said. "I can help."

Mama shook her head. "You have your pa and Abe to look after, Sally. Do your duty and mind them both."

I walked along the path a ways with Mama, kicking through the leaves, carrying her basket on my shoulder. I would have toted it all the way for her. A stone of worry filled my insides. I didn't want her to go, but I didn't say nothing. It was my foolishness. Mama always went to help when a neighbor ailed, and this was Aunt Betsy. So I went on chirping like a bird, giving Mama a cheerful send-off.

We said good-bye by the big hollow tree where the road edged our land. Mama took her basket and strode off. All of a sudden, I ran after her and I cried out again, "Mama. Good-bye!" She turned and smiled a little and waved me back. "Good-bye," I called. "Good-bye, Mama!"

CHAPTER 17

Tremblin' Country

*M*ama didn't come back the next day or the day after, either. With her gone, I was doing every minute, freshening the beds, taking care of the fire, cooking, milking, and sweeping out the cabin. There weren't no end to the chores, and it chafed me, was I doing things proper? I needed Mama here to guide my hand. Besides, it was more'n I wanted to do. There was never a moment to sit down or fun around with Abe.

"What's the long face you got on you, Sally?" Pa asked, when I was putting out supper food the second day.

"No long face," I said, being very pert and irritable. "And, Abe, don't you say nothing about me burning the squash, neither!"

"I didn't say nothing," Abe said.

"Well, don't!" I sat down with a thud. I didn't even want to eat.

Next morning, a pig herder stopped by to deliver a message to us and Pa. He was a stocky, rough-talking man. He and his dog were herding a mess of pigs fanned out across the road. "Mrs. Lincoln says to say her aunt Betsy Sparrow have the puking sickness bad." The herder man snapped his whip at a pig. "Mrs. Lincoln says to say she'd be staying longer."

Pa took his hat off and slammed it down into the dirt.

"How long is Mama staying?" I said. "Is she coming home tomorrow?"

The pig herder looked down at me. "Now, how would I know that?"

Pa picked up his hat and rubbed his head hard before he put it on again. "How bad has Mrs. Sparrow got the puking sickness?"

"Bad," the pig herder said. "She ain't the only one. It's showing in most every farm I passed, animals trembling, people puking. I'll sure be glad to be clear of this country. When I get over on the Kentucky side, it'll be a whole lot better. Ain't nothing like this Indiana territory. This here is tremblin' country."

He whistled to his dog to bring the foraging pigs back

to the road. The hogs started to holler and protest, but the herder snapped his whip, and he and his dog got the hogs moving and went on.

I'd been listening to everything, but I wasn't truly hearing, because I was in a froth just thinking about another day of doing everything without Mama. I wanted Mama back here *now*. Abe was hopping around, like he didn't even care. Made me so mad I almost didn't hear Pa.

He was looking away, shading his eyes, like he saw someone coming. "I don't know when," he said slow, almost like he was speaking to himself, "but I'm thinking Aunt Betsy Sparrow's going to need a box and a resting place."

That brought me up some. "Pa? You think Aunt Betsy's going to pass?"

"I heard it said praying helps, Sal, but I don't know about that. The shaking sickness takes people faster than a leaf in a flood."

All the rest of the morning, Pa and Abe worked on splitting boards out of sawed pine logs, then setting them up with spacers to dry. Noontime, I fixed meat and bread and some hocks and greens, and I didn't burn nothing. I was doing everything slow and careful, thinking of Mama, but not in a temper anymore. Just wanting her home with us.

After he ate, Pa set to building a coffin out of the drying boards. Late afternoon, he and Abe loaded the box on the wagon and Pa hitched up the horses. The birds were singing their sunset songs. Bats were swooping by. Pa packed pine splits to light his way in the dark and climbed up on the seat.

"Let me and Abe come with you, Pa," I said. "We can help you and Mama. And we'll say good-bye to Aunt Betsy."

"No, Sal." Pa's chin was set. "You both got your chores to do. I'm going to fetch your mama home." Pa laid his rifle at his feet and clicked his tongue at the horses, and they set off.

The light was going out of the sky and the woods were black. Abe and me went inside. It was real strange being alone in the cabin, just the two of us. The firelight flickered across my brother's face. The corners of the cabin were all shadowy and dark. Where was Mama now? I wished I was with her, bustling around, making Aunt Betsy comfortable. A shiver went down my back and I shook my shoulders, thinking I could hear Mama crying for Aunt Betsy.

"Abe," I said. "You afeared?"

"No. No, no, no." He sank down near the fire "Are you afeared?"

"I didn't say that!" I looked out the window hole, hoping for some angel of light to come fluttering down and drive away my gloomy thoughts. Abe took the Bible from the shelf and spread it open on his lap. I lit a candle, and he read out loud to comfort us.

CHAPTER 18

Mama, Where Are You?

Late the next day, Pa came back, but he was alone. "Where's Mama?" I left off scrubbing the table. "Is she outside?" I went to the door and looked out into the yard. Abe was patting down the horses. His face was all twisted up. "What's the matter with Abe?" I said, looking around for Mama.

"He's fretting," Pa said. "Your aunt Betsy passed last night."

"Oh!" I sank down onto a stool. "Aunt Betsy," I mumbled, trying not to cry. "Oh, Aunt Betsy." I sat there, my head drooping, thinking of all the things I loved about Aunt Betsy, how kind she was to everyone, even her grumpy husband, how she cooked the best apple fritters, and how she made Mama laugh with her stories.

Pa laid a hand on my head, for a moment only, but it was real tender. "This morning," he said, "your mama and me laid your aunt Betsy out in the box I brought."

"Where's Mama now?" I said.

Pa sat down at the table. "What have you got for me to eat, Sal? I didn't have nothing but a mouthful of corn pone before I set out. Your mama? She's still there. I couldn't persuade her to come home where she belongs."

I put down some cold meat and bread in front of Pa. "Don't she miss us, like we miss her?"

Pa chewed on the bread. "Her uncle Sparrow is failing now. He couldn't raise his self up from the bed this morning. It's the milk sickness, all right. I told your mama there's nothing to do but get clear of it, and she knows it, but there's no moving her when she has a duty to perform."

"Mama's good," I said.

"Too good," Pa grunted. "She said she knew the Lord wanted her there to care for her uncle Sparrow and young Hanks, too."

"Is Dennis also sick?" I said.

"No, I didn't say that. Not yet, anyway. And don't you go crying, Sal. It's useless to cry."

"I know that, Pa. I'm sorry." I wiped my eyes on my sleeve.

That night, I knelt and prayed for Mama and Uncle Sparrow and our cousin Dennis Hanks. "Lord, I know You say who lives and who dies. I know whatever happens, we are but as a glove on Your hand. You can put this glove on or take it off as You see fit. I know I should be humble and not ask for things, but I want Mama here. Please, Lord, keep her safe and send her home."

Maybe I didn't pray loud enough for the Lord to hear. It was eight days more before I saw Mama again. In that time, Pa made the trip to the Sparrow homestead twice more. Once, to dig the grave and bury Aunt Betsy Sparrow and the second time, a few days later, after he and Abe finished making another coffin box, to carry it over for Uncle Sparrow.

Sitting by the fire that night with Pa gone, Abe and me talked about Aunt Betsy and Uncle Sparrow. "Are you sorrowing for Uncle Sparrow?" Abe asked.

"I expect I am." I poked at the fire. Truth was, try hard as I would, I couldn't find but a tear or maybe two in my heart for that man. "I didn't hate him, but I didn't love him neither. Now he's gone to be with Aunt Betsy."

"We know a lot of dead people," Abe said slowly.

"Abe." I poked up the fire some more and thought of something to cheer him. "Cousin Dennis is going to come live with us now. Pa'll be fetching him along with Mama."

Two mornings later, Pa was back. Snow was falling,

big, fat, soft flakes covering everything like the best white linen. Cousin Dennis was sitting up next to Pa. "Look, Abe. Didn't I tell you Dennis was coming?"

"Where's Mama?" Abe said.

I ran toward the wagon. Pa pushed his hand through the air, as if he wanted me to stay away. Mama was lying in back, covered with a blanket. "Mama?" I said. Her eyes fluttered open. She looked at me, but she didn't say anything. "Mama!" Her skin was waxy pale.

"Hush, Sally." Pa wiped at his eyes and got down from the wagon. He and Cousin Dennis lifted Mama and carried her toward the cabin. I ran ahead and smoothed the bed. They laid her down and Abe pulled the quilt over her.

"Watch over your mama, children," Pa said, and he and Dennis went outside to take care of the animals.

Mama motioned for me to take the horn comb out of her hair. "Keep it," she whispered.

"I'll put it under your pillow for you, Mama."

"No . . . no . . . it's yours . . . now . . . it's yours. . . ." Her eyes were sunk down.

"Mama," I choked. "Mama. When you're better, I'll comb your hair and you'll wear your comb."

"Sally." She was breathing harsh. "Keep it," she said again in that little voice I'd never heard before. "I want you to have . . . it."

"All right, Mama." I held the comb to my lips, then put it into my pocket.

"Where's my Abe?" Mama said, her eyes searching for him. "Abe . . ." She reached out for his hand and then mine. "No fear, children. Trust in the Lord, I'm just . . ."—her voice faded—"tired. . . ." Her eyes closed.

"You rest, Mama," Abe said.

"Yes, rest, Mama, I can do everything," I said. "All the while you've been gone, Pa never had to correct me nor Abe. Never a squabble. Not a single unkind word." I couldn't tell if she heard me. I think she was asleep already.

Later, when dark came, I stepped outside and talked quiet to the Lord. I stood under His starry glitter, looking up, and promised Him that if He would just make Mama well again, I would change my ways. I would banish all my wicked thoughts and speech, I would be kinder to my brother, and never speak up to sass Pa again. I would do it all if He would save Mama.

That night, Pa stayed by Mama in his chair, a quilt over his shoulders, and I lay on the hearth, my back to the fire, holding Mama's comb. I wanted to stay awake should she need me, but the hearthstone was warm, and I couldn't keep my eyes from shutting. In the morning, it was Mama's puking that woke me.

━━ CHAPTER 19 ━━

Where's My Abe?

All that week, I slept on the hearth. Off and on, through the darkness, I'd hear Mama moaning or Pa talking low to her. Days, I made healing teas for her, the way she'd taught me. At first, I was in a dither. I kept asking Mama, "Is the tea good? Is it too strong? Did I put in enough mint? Enough elder?" Sometimes she'd nod and try to smile. Sometimes she'd sip, then shake her head for me to take it away.

She was burning with fever, puking, and hardly eating. I tried to cool her. I wiped her face and her arms and legs with a wet cloth. When she puked, I cleaned her up and emptied the basin. I didn't want to leave her, and I didn't, not ever, except for necessity.

Sometimes, Abe came in from working with Pa and Cousin Dennis and went over to Mama's bed and stood by her. He didn't say nothing, just looked at her and looked at her.

Late one afternoon, neighbor women stopped by, three of them in a two-wheeled cart harnessed to a donkey. The donkey was wearing a bonnet, and the ladies all wore bonnets too. One lady, tall and thin, with a frowning kind of face, got down from the wagon and went inside to see Mama.

"That's Mrs. John Crawford," the lady holding the reins said to me. "She's a midwife, and she knows all about healing. She'll fix up your mama. Are you the daughter?"

"Yes, ma'am, that's me."

"What's your name?"

"Sarah," I said, "but most everyone calls me Sally."

"And a good thing they do," she said. "Call out *Sarah* in these parts, and near every female in ten miles looks around."

Mrs. Crawford came hurrying out. "It's the trembles," she said, climbing into the wagon.

"Yes, ma'am, that's what Pa said."

Mrs. Crawford looked down at me, "Do you know how to make healing teas for your mama?"

"Yes, ma'am, I do that."

"Well . . . well . . ." Frowning, she clasped her hands. "Keep doing it. I can't do nothing else for your mama. I'm sorry."

The lady holding the reins clicked her tongue at the donkey, and they drove away, the donkey's hooves scattering the fallen leaves.

I kept on making teas and thin gruel for Mama, but she didn't want any of it. She wanted water, just water. When she spoke in that small weak voice, it was only to ask for water. One morning, she couldn't get her eyes open, couldn't even lift her head a tad to take a sip of water. She slept, her breathing loud and gasping. Sometime midmorning, she woke and called out for Abe. "Abe. Where's my Abe?"

I bent over her. "I'll get him, Mama. I'll get him for you." I ran outside. He was in the field with Pa and Cousin Dennis, all of them bundling up the hay. "Mama wants you, Abe," I cried.

"Me?"

"Hurry!"

In the house, he went close to the bed. "Mama, I'm here," he said. "I'm here. I'm here." Mama's hand wavered up out of the cover, and Abe took it and held it.

"Listen to your . . . father," Mama gasped. "He loves

you. Be . . ."—she paused, her breath came short and hard—"respectful."

"Yes, Mama," he said. Tears ran down his face.

The next morning, when I woke up, Mama lay still on the bed. That day was the fifth day of the month of October, the year of our Lord 1818. That was a day I would never forget. When I touched Mama's face, she was cold. "Mama?" I grabbed her hands. I kissed them. I kissed her cheeks. I kissed her lips. Cold. Cold. Cold. "Mama," I cried. "Mama, talk to me. Where are you?"

Not here, the silence said. Not here. No more.

I ran outside. I ran past Pa, who was measuring a board; I ran past Abe, who was holding the board steady; I ran past Cousin Dennis, coming back from the spring with a bucket of water in each big hand. I ran round the corner of the house. I didn't know where I was going. I was running, just running, looking for Mama.

"Mama, where are you?" I screamed.

Not in the garden and not where she liked to sit in the shade of the trees, working at the wheel. Only the calf was there, and she reached up and licked my face so tender, as if she knew.

"Mama says nobody stays," I told the calf. I was crying and talking and looking up at the sky, and trying to laugh, too, remembering the rhyme Mama made up.

"Company comes, but it's just for a day. Here they come, don't want to stay. Look around, look at the sun, and—" My voice faltered. I threw my arms around the calf, buried my face in her smooth skin, and finished Mama's rhyme. "Look around, look at the sun, and . . . and . . . and away they've run."

CHAPTER 20

Tears Like Rain

We buried Mama on the hill above our cabin. Pa dragged the coffin on a sled, and we all took turns digging the grave. I wasn't much use, I was crying too much. Pa didn't cry, nor did Cousin Dennis Hanks, nor Abe, neither. After that, every day was like all the days before, except Mama wasn't with us. Sometimes I pretended she was still over visiting Aunt Betsy and would be stepping back any moment.

I looked for signs everywhere that she would be returned to me. When Lightning coughed, I prayed it was a sign. When I found a snakeskin, and when the moon was new, I prayed the grave away. When I stepped outside, I wouldn't look at the hill and that dark mound of earth. And when the wolves howled at night, I buried my head under the quilt and begged them to find Mama and bring her back to me.

If Pa caught me grieving, he said, "Sal, what is, is, and what will be, will be, and no tears of yours can reverse God's decree. The best you can do is to remember your mama and walk in her footsteps."

"Yes, Pa," I said, but I couldn't stop my heart from wanting Mama.

Shortly after we laid Mama to rest, Pa hitched up Branch and dragged a big square rock from Pigeon Creek and laid it down at the door to the cabin. Months ago, Mama and I had found that rock half-buried at the edge of the creek. Mama had clapped her hands joyfully. "There's our threshold stone, Sally." Pa had promised to move it, but he'd never found the time. Just before she went to care for Aunt Betsy, Mama had said, "Sally, we're not going to wait for your pa. You and I are going to walk that stone to our cabin ourselves, no matter if it takes us all day."

No need for us to do it, Mama. Look! Here's your rock, setting pretty, just where you wanted it. There it was, smooth and solid as could be, for us all to step on as we entered the cabin. There it was in the doorway where she and I would sit mornings, warmed by the sun, Mama spinning and me sewing or mixing the corn for our mealtime bread.

There it was, waiting for the lilac bush she planned on putting in, come next spring. *Mama, I'll put that lilac bush in the ground. I promise you I will.*

Days went by, then weeks. Winter came. Evenings, Abe sat by the fire, not talking, not whittling, mostly just reading. Sometimes he raised his head, like the dogs did when they caught a scent in the air, and his eyes went all around the cabin, then dropped again to his book. He didn't talk about Mama. Nor did Pa.

A Reverend Mr. Elkins, a minister from back in Kentucky who knew Mama and Pa, came to Indiana territory to visit his son. When he heard that Mama had died without a proper burial, he stopped by us and spoke over her grave. I stood there leaning against Pa and holding Abe's hand.

"Now your hearts can rest." Reverend Mr. Elkins concluded his sermon, but my heart had never rested since Mama died. I was thinking again about my little baby brother, Thomas, laying in the ground at the Knob Creek farm. I was thinking how, when we visited his grave, Mama would kneel and murmur, "Dear God, I know we are but sojourners in this sad world. We hold our blessings with trembling hands and thank You for each day that You give us." That was what Mama would want me to do now, and I tried. I did! I truly tried to be thankful, but I longed so for Mama that the tears still spilled from me like rain that wouldn't let up.

I went on sleeping downstairs in sight of Mama and Pa's bed. Pa made an underbed for me, and every night, I pulled it out from beneath the bed in the corner, and every morning, I pushed it back. And each and every time the thought came over me of Mama lying there so sick and weak.

Abe and Dennis had the sleeping platform now. They did everything together; if you saw one, you saw the other. Abe was almost half-Dennis in years, but he was already two hands taller, and he could hold his own with stories and jokes. Nights, I'd hear them talking, Dennis's deep voice, Abe's higher. After they fell silent and Pa started in snoring, I'd still be lying wakeful, thinking of Mama.

Days were better. Now that I had to do all that Mama had done, I had no time for crying or wishing or feeling poorly. Mornings, I hurried to freshen the fire and milk the cow. Then it was time to cook. Abe and Dennis could put away a heap of food. It was johnnycake and three kinds of meat at every meal. After that, there was the washing up and sweeping and fetching water and wood. I was always busy, and so was Abe. Still, I wished he would talk about Mama, or that Pa would.

Pa never even said Mama's name. Had he forgotten all about her? He was always going from one chore to another, taking down trees and cutting wood, always fixing to improve this or that on the farm, the land or the fences or the root cellar. When he said anything, it was sure to be a sermon about work. "We got no place here for idlers. Chores don't do themselves. If you're going to wear out your clothes, wear them out doing something useful. *Be useful!* Let that be your scripture. A day when you don't do something for your family is a day lost."

The winter passed, and still my thoughts flew through my heart to Mama. Many nights I'd wake all of a sudden, thinking I heard her calling me. I'd sit up and listen, waiting to hear her voice again. Waiting and waiting.

Spring came, and I found a wild lilac and dug it out and planted it near our door. That night, Mama came to me in my dreams, and we held hands and walked along the trace to the creek. The next morning, I woke up happy.

CHAPTER 21

Sorry Is As Sorry Does

$\mathcal{M}$any days, Abe and Dennis did the plowing, while Pa was off doing carpentry for folks. Everyone knew that Pa made good sturdy furniture and hung doors real straight. He was mostly paid in trade. One time he come home with two hens and a rooster, and we had eggs from then on.

He made us a door, too, traded a table to the blacksmith for nails and metal hinges. He threw the bear skin that had been hanging in the door opening down on the floor. That was a real comfort to the feet. "We got us a door," Pa said, rubbing his hands together and, for once, smiling. He opened and closed the door, time upon time, and then he had each of us, Dennis, Abe, and me, open and close it too.

"That's a fine door, Uncle Thomas," Dennis said.

"Yes, it is," Pa said. He was so proud of that door! And yet never did he mention Mama and how she had longed for a door, waited so patiently for it. If only she could have been here to see it, been the first one to open and close it.

Many months had passed since Mama had left us, and I tried to keep a cheerful heart. In the cabin, I did the best I knew how, but seemed as if too often I'd be doing one thing and spoiling something else. Came a morning in June, I let the fire get too hot and scorched the meat, and while I was tending to that, the milk boiled over.

"Sal," Pa said, "ain't you never going to learn to do things proper?"

"Sorry, Pa. I'm trying." I swiped my arm across my forehead.

"Sorry is as sorry does. You got working men here; they need their food on time and cooked proper."

"I know that, Pa."

"Well, then, learn to do it right!"

Tears welled up in my eyes. "Yes, Pa. I'll try harder."

"You crying? Just sit down and eat."

I sat down. I put meat and johnnycake on my plate, but I couldn't hardly swallow a bite. My head sank down to the table and I cried out Mama's name.

"Sally," Pa said. "Lift your head up, girl."

"I can't stand it no more," I sobbed. "I don't want to live without Mama."

"Sally!" Pa knuckled the table. "Be your mama's daughter. She had iron in her blood. She never let go."

I wiped my eyes and swallowed back the tears. With all my heart, I wanted to be my mama's daughter, but so much sorrow was in me it bent my legs and made a noise in my head. I sat at the table, staring at my hands.

Pa finished his meal and stood up. "Sally, you haven't eaten a bite. Don't throw that food away." He went out, taking Dennis with him.

"Sally," Abe said.

I didn't answer.

"Sally, you going to talk to me?"

I shook my head.

"I got a secret for you."

"I don't want your secret. I don't want to hear anything. I don't want to see you or nobody." I sank my face into my hands. "Nobody cares that Mama's gone. You don't care, Abe, I know you don't. It makes me want to die. I want to die and be with Mama."

"Sally, Mama's here," Abe said. "I see her all the time."

I looked up. "No, you don't. She's in heaven and her

body's in the ground. Right up there on the hill."

Abe moved closer and took my arm. "Mama's here, watching over us. You told me yourself souls never die. Mama's soul is flying around and she's talking to me."

"No," I cried out. My belly hurt. Why did Mama's soul talk to Abe and not to me?

"Mama says you're good, Sally, and for me to look after you and not let you do anything like dying."

"You're making it up, Abraham. That's a whopper and you're a liar. Mama would never say that. She gave *you* to *me* to look after. She gave *you* to *me*, when you were nothing but just a wriggling ugly little worm. Now you think you're all growed up, just because you're friends with Dennis! Now you say anything that comes into your head. You hop around and make Dennis laugh. You make up stories, and Mama is just another story to you."

His face puffed up. He was shaking. "No, Sally. You're wrong." He took my hands in his. "I will look after you, like Mama told me. I won't let nothing and nobody hurt you. Dennis—" He shook his head. "That's just larking."

"Abe." I felt so bad that I'd said those things, but happy, too, because now I knew we were sorrowing over Mama together. I got my arms around him. He was my little brother, but I had to reach up to embrace him.

Later, we went up the hill to where Mama lay in the ground. We cleared around the mound, then gathered handfuls of grass and leaves and covered her over with them like a warm blanket.

CHAPTER 22

A Letter for Pa

$\mathscr{I}$ was getting ready to hang out the wash one hot August day when a boy on horseback came through the trees. It was so hot my shift stuck to my skin. The leaves were curling up on the trees and dropping to the ground. The boy was shirtless, a blue rag tied around his head.

I took the wooden pins out of my mouth and said, "Howdy! Looks like you could use a drink."

"This here where Thomas Lincoln lives?"

No howdy. No manners. Didn't even dismount. Sitting there above me as if I was lower than a bug on the ground.

"You got ears?" the boy said.

He was a fair bit older than me.

"Girl, this where Thomas Lincoln lives?"

"Who are you?" I stuck my hands on my hips. "I never seen you before. You ain't from around here."

"Shows how much you know." He fished a letter out of his pack. "Where can I find Mr. Thomas Lincoln?"

"Give it here." I put out my hand. "I'm his daughter."

"I been instructed to deliver it *personally* to Mr. Thomas Lincoln."

We eyed each other kind of unfriendly, then I went around to where Pa and Abe were fixing to make a hollow stump into a corncrib. "Pa," I said. "Someone here with a letter for you."

"Who's that?"

"He didn't say his name. He's a rude fellow, Pa."

Pa put his saw down and came back around with me. "Howdy," he said to the boy, who was really almost a man. "Sure is hot."

"Sure is," the boy-man said. "You Mr. Thomas Lincoln?"

"Depends," Pa said. "What's your business with him?"

"I brought a letter for Mr. Thomas Lincoln from Mrs. Sarah Bush Johnston in Elizabethtown, Kentucky."

"Is that right?" Pa said. "You telling me you came all that way just to bring Thomas Lincoln a letter?"

"No, sir, I also came back to visit my family. I been several years working for my uncle over there, but I'm from around here."

"What's your name?"

"Aaron Grigsby." He took the blue rag off his head and wiped his face. His eyes were almost the same blue color as the rag.

"Sally," Pa said, "where's your manners? Get this boy some water."

I brought him the pail and the dipper. He drank like he hadn't had a sip of water in a week. "Mighty grateful, Sally," he said, handing me back the dipper.

Imagine! Saying my name like that, like he knew me. I tossed my braid back over my shoulder and went to stand alongside Pa.

"You one of Rueben Grigsby's boys?" Pa said.

"Yes, sir, I am."

"Well, I know your father, and you can give me the letter, because I'm Tom Lincoln."

"Thought so," Aaron Grigsby said, and handed over the letter. Then he tied the rag around his head again and left.

Pa was examining the letter, looking at it front and back. Then he started in making as if he could read, his lips moving like it was blab school, and he was sounding the words out loud. "My . . . dear . . . Mr. Lincoln."

"Pa," I said. "Let me read it for you."

"Fetch your brother. I'll have Abe read it," Pa said. "He can read better than you."

"No, Pa! I can read good as him. You know I can. Anyway, he's busy."

Frowning, Pa gave me the letter. "Read it, and don't mumble, Sally."

"I won't, Pa."

"Read it slow."

"Yes, Pa."

"Slow and plain, so as I can take it all in."

I cleared my throat, stood straight, and began.

My dear Mr. Lincoln,

Forgive me for not Corresponding sooner, but the News of your dear Wife Nancy Hanks Lincoln's passing last year only now reached me. You can imagine with what Disbelief and Sorrow I received the dreadful News. I learned of it from the Reverend Mr. Elkins, whose Church he said you and Mrs. Lincoln once attended. He recently stopped to Visit and brought me the sad News. He is also writing this letter for me, as perhaps you Know I am

not good with lettering. Reverend Mr.
Elkins relays to me that your Dear Wife
was buried without a Proper Christian
service and that some months later he
preached over her grave and gave her
over to our Precious Lord. I believe this
must have been of great Comfort to you.

It has been many years since my Dearest
Nancy and I were girls together in
Elizabethtown. Nancy was like the Best
Older sister to me, Always loving and
caring. So many years have Passed that
we haven't seen each other, but the
Precious Memories remain. I can still see
her Bright Loving Face, how she laughed,
how she loved to Dance. Oh, my Nancy!
She has never been out of my Thoughts,
and our few letters Exchanged are among
my most precious Possessions.

Dear Mr. Lincoln, our lives, although
Years and Miles apart, have gone along
somewhat parallel paths, joined by
Fate and God in so many Ways. You
married dear Nancy only Months after
my marriage to Daniel Johnston. My

firstborn, Elizabeth, like your firstborn, is
a daughter, and they are close in Age. My
next born was also a daughter, Matilda.
And lastly, a boy, John, now age ten.
And you, too, have a boy, I hear, much
the same age. And now we have both
Suffered the Loss of our spouses.

I will say Truthfully, however, your
marriage has been so much Happier and
Longer than mine was. Whatever the
Difficulties of my own life, it was always
a great comfort to know that my Dear
Nancy thrived, and that you and your
precious remaining children were well.

Dear Mr. Lincoln, my brothers all
remember themselves to you Affectionately
and Join me in extending their great
sympathy at your loss. My brother Isaac
Particularly wants you to know that
he still thinks with great joy of your
Adventuring on the Mississippi! He asks
do you Remember, as he does, how the Two
of you rafted a load of goods down to New
Orleans? I informed him that I was sure

you remembered it all very well! Three months you were gone and returned just after my marriage to Mr. Johnston, each of you with a present for me! I still have the metal washbasin you brought me. It has been in Use these many years.

How happy we all were then! How little we Knew. Death spares no one. We move through life as if in a Dream, not knowing our Fate. All rests in the Lord's hands, and Bow we must to His will. But whatever our Fate, we remain grateful for our portion, Thankful for our infants who have survived and for each day we are given. Dear Mr. Lincoln, late as these words come and Conscious as I am that they are wholly Inadequate to express the depths of my Grief at the Passing of your dear wife, I remain grateful that I am able to send them. I send this letter with the Hope that it finds you and your dear children Well and Strong.

I remain your Devoted Friend,
Sarah Bush Johnston.

It was a long letter! When I finished, I took a deep breath and handed it to Pa. "Thankee, Sally," he said. He slowly folded the letter. "Your mama and me knew Sarah Bush back in Kentucky. Knew her and her brother Isaac before she was Sarah Johnston."

"Were you sweet on her, Pa?"

"What a mouth you got on you, Sally!"

"Well, were you, Pa?" I giggled, and Pa almost smiled.

➤ CHAPTER 23 ➤

Your Mama Would Agree

*A*utumn came, leaves were turning, and nights were getting cold. The last week in September, a steady cold rain drove us all inside. I had stew heating on the fire. Cousin Dennis had been hunting and keeping us in meat. Pa went out to make sure the animals were under cover. When he came back in, the water dripping off his hat and coat, he went right to the fire to dry.

"Uncle Thomas," Dennis said. "Got to tell you something."

"What's that?" Pa turned himself to dry his backside.

"I'll be going off to work for wages on the Peabody farm."

"Peabody farm!" Pa said. "That's a day's journey from here."

Cousin Dennis nodded. "Giving me room and board and a wage, too."

"Well." Pa turned again and rubbed his hands over his face. "Better'n I can do. Might as well go."

Two days later, when Cousin Dennis left, Pa gave him Lightning to make his trip easier. "You be good," I whispered in her ear. "Don't kick nobody."

I missed Lightning, but Abe missed Cousin Dennis, and so did Pa. His going left them both low. From the day we saw him off, it seemed as if nothing suited Pa anymore. Used to be that he was severe with Abe and tolerated me, but now, wherever he looked he saw something wrong with Abe's work and with mine, too.

The night of October 5, it was a Tuesday and a year to the day since Mama left us. We were all in by the fire. That afternoon, Abe and I had gone to her grave again and talked to her and prayed together. Now we were trying to be peaceful, Abe reading, me mending my shift. I kept looking at Pa, though. He was aiming to fix a boot, but not doing it, just sitting and gazing around the cabin, his eyes stopping on all the places where I'd dropped things, on the unaired bedding and the clothes waiting to be washed.

"How much can a body endure?" he muttered.

I dropped my mending. My throat ached. Part of me

wanted to say, *I'm sorry, Pa. I am sorry!* But the sinful part of me just didn't want to do that! Wasn't there cooked meat on the table at every meal? And fish and boiled greens and hog fat? And didn't I know how to leach lye out of ashes and make soap, and wasn't the soap gourd kept filled? The candles I dipped were never as straight as Mama's, but didn't they burn and give good light? I knew I wasn't as good as Mama and never would be. Nobody had to tell me that, but I was doing better all the time.

Abe looked up from his book. Maybe he saw my long face and guessed what I was thinking, because he spoke up to Pa. "Tell us a story, Pa. Tell us about the pirates and how you went down the Mississippi on that flatboat."

"Yes, Pa, do," I got out. It always cheered Pa to yarn awhile. "Tell us how you and Mama got married, and how you came back from New Orleans with your pockets full of coins, and you had a suit made special, and you wore a beaver hat."

"Leave me be." Pa started in sewing the boot. "I don't have no heart for storytelling these days."

Then we were all quiet, until it was time to bed down. Next day, Abe and me found a chance to talk about Pa. "I never seen him so low," I said.

"Lower'n a snake's belly," Abe said.

"Maybe Cousin Dennis will be coming back soon." I was sure that Pa's low spirits were on account of Dennis's being gone, but I was wrong.

Some weeks later, toward the end of the month, I was brooming the floor after we ate, when Pa suddenly said, "Sally fetch me the Bible. I want Abe to read Mrs. Sarah Bush Johnston's letter to me."

I took the Bible off the shelf and brought it to Pa. "Why do you want Abe to read it to you? I already did that!"

"That was a good while back, Sal." He opened the book and took out Mrs. Johnston's letter. "I'm needful of hearing it again."

"Pa! Didn't you listen when I was reading it?"

"Sally," he said, "you're mouthy enough for three! I know your mama taught you better than that. You need some taming down, girl."

"Sorry, Pa," I mumbled. I set aside the broom and sat down with a pan of unshelled peas in my lap. Pa was right about me being mouthy. Mama used to correct me on that. I sat there, shelling peas, only half-listening to Abe reading Mrs. Johnston's letter, promising myself to be more respectful and quiet and not always be saying what I was thinking.

When Abe was done reading, Pa sat for a bit, then

said, "Abraham. Sarah. It's more'n a year since your mama passed, and it hasn't been easy for me. This house needs a woman and you children need a mother."

"No, Pa," I burst out, already forgetting my promise to myself. "We already have a mother. We can't have another one."

"Listen to me, Sally. And you, too, Abe. A man can't properly raise young 'uns by himself." He folded the letter away inside the covers of the Bible. "My work is outside, and the house is a woman's place. It takes a woman to teach and correct and raise you up righteously."

Abe and me looked at each other. "Yes, Pa," we both said. Neither one of us meant it.

Just two nights later, when I thought he'd forgotten about it, Pa went back to the subject of new mamas and Sarah Bush Johnston. He'd put Abe to braiding the end of a hank of rope, and he'd settled down to finishing a stool he was making for one of our neighbors. "Children, I been thinking," he said, and Abe and I both looked up.

"Been thinking about Mrs. Sarah Bush Johnston, who used to be plain Sarah Bush. I knowed all the Bushes, her and her brothers and her father. Good folks. Sarah's father was my captain when I was patrolling the roads. Your mama and I both knowed Sarah since she was a slip of a girl. We also knowed Daniel Johnston before they got married, and we never had much use for him."

He set the stool down and told me to try it. I sat down on it. "Steady as a rock, Pa. Why didn't you and Mama like Daniel Johnston?"

"He was a great one for borrowing and 'forgetting' to pay. He lost everything Sarah Bush brought him, everything that her father had given her. They weren't poor to start out, but he left her a poor widow with nothing to her name but three children."

"Elizabeth, Matilda, and John," I said. Those names had stayed in my head.

"That's right," Pa said, and then, real casual, he added, "I been thinking, those children of hers need a father. And Sarah Johnston would be a good mother for you two. Your mama would agree."

CHAPTER 24

This Here Is Tom Lincoln

Before the week was out, Pa brought home a length of cloth that he'd traded at Grigsby's store and handed it to me. "I need a shirt," he said, "and Abe can use one too. And you need a new shift."

"Don't know if I can do all that, Pa," I said. "I can make a shift, but I don't know about the shirts."

He slapped down his hand. "That's what I been saying, Sally! You need a mama. I can't teach you how to make a shirt."

He had brought something else from Grigsby's too, an envelope and paper. That caught Abe's attention. "Is that for me, Pa?" He was forever wanting paper to practice his lettering.

"No, it ain't for you, Abe. This paper has a purpose.

Sit down, Sally, we're going to write a letter." He set the paper in front of me and took the inkwell off the shelf. It was half-full of blue elderberry ink that Abe had made. "Start the proper way," Pa said. "You know. 'My dear Mrs. Sarah Bush Johnston. This here is Tom Lincoln inquiring about your health and happiness, using the Good Services of my daughter, Sarah, also known as Sally, to put down these words.'"

I wrote carefully, trying not to think about what I was writing *or* drip ink on the paper. "Ready, Pa." I held the quill over the inkwell, waiting for his next words.

"Well, go on," he said. "You know what I'm going to say to her."

"No, I don't, Pa." That was almost a lie.

"I don't beat around the bush. I'm a plainspoken man, and I'm going to say it plain and honest. 'Mrs. Johnston, you need somebody. I need somebody. What more has to be said? Two horses pulling together can move a load easier than one.'"

"Two horses! Is that what you said to our mama when you were courting her?"

"Never mind that, Sally. Just write it down."

I wrote, "Mrs. Johnston, you need somebody." Then I stopped. I could just let Pa go his own stubborn way, but something in me wanted to protect him. "Pa?" I said. "I don't think a lady wants to hear that she's a horse."

"I didn't say she was a horse! She'll know what I mean. It's a hard life, we've both had misfortune, and we both have children to raise. A man and a woman need each other. Write that down. Write that I need a mother for my children, and I'm ready to be a father to hers."

He watched while I wrote it all, made the letters that made the words that made a sentence that set my heart to beating too hard and made my eyes water up. I was helping Pa ask a stranger woman to be our mama. ". . . and ready to be a father to yours," I wrote. "Done, Pa."

"Good, Sally. Now say, 'Your children and mine together will make us both a fine family.'"

I dipped the pen, shook off the extra ink, and wrote it.

"Now write, 'I'm proposing that we team up, you and me, Sarah Bush Johnston and Tom Lincoln, and that we continue down the road of life together and take whatever God will give us.'"

That night, listening to Pa's snores and Abe's mutterings in his sleep, I whispered into my covers, talking to Mama, like I did most every night. *Mama, you always told me to obey and honor Pa, so you know I had to write that letter.* I took her pretty comb out from under my pillow where I kept it next to Amanda, and kissed them both, so I could sleep peaceful.

CHAPTER 25

One Question

$\mathcal{P}$a rode out to Troy to post the letter to Mrs. Sarah Bush Johnston. "I expect I'll get her answer right quick," he said. "I give her a week." He was whistling every day that week. On the Sabbath, he sat us down and said, "I want you children to listen close. Me and our neighbors been talking to Mr. Andrew Crawford, the justice of the peace, and he's agreeable to having a school this winter. You remember last summer, we built him that log schoolhouse just south of us?"

"I remember! I talked to Mr. Crawford, and I seen the school," Abe said, his eyes all lit up. "Did you see it, Sally?" He jumped up, then sat down, then jumped up again, so excited he couldn't stay still. "It's a fine place!"

"I ain't seen it yet," I said. "I guess I will sometime."

"Yes, you will," Pa said, "because you're going there, starting in December. Less'n a month. I put down hard cash and subscribed both of you."

"Pa!" Abe said. "Thankee!"

Were it up to Abe, he'd have been in school every day of the year. I liked learning, too, but not near as much as he did.

"Mr. Crawford is an upstanding, educated man," Pa went on. "I want you to listen to him and learn. I don't intend my children to grow up ignorant like me. I never went to school."

"Yes, Pa," Abe and I said almost together.

"I was a laboring boy from when I was but six years old."

"Yes, Pa," we said again. We'd heard all this before.

"My mama needed what little I earned." He went on with his story, telling us again about growing up without a pa, and how he saw his pa cut down by Indians. He was in a fine reminiscing mood. I hadn't heard him jaw like that since Mama died. He looked real pleased with himself, too, *because of Mrs. Johnston,* I thought, and I couldn't get excited like Abe about school.

"Sal," Abe said, "Mr. Crawford told me I could borrow any of his books I wanted."

"I know that, Abe," I said. "You told me that already.

Two times you told me. This makes three. Don't always be telling me the same thing, Abraham, I got other things to think about."

Mrs. Johnston's letter didn't come that week, nor the next. I hoped it would never come. I even prayed to God, which was sinful. I knew Mama would say you should never pray for things to go wrong for somebody else. Anyway, the letter finally came—only it wasn't from Mrs. Johnston. It was from two of her brothers.

Pa gave me the letter to read aloud to him, and I can tell you there weren't no chatting in it, and nothing soft like Mrs. Johnston's letter to Pa. Her brothers had a question for Pa, and there weren't no easing up to the subject. Just:

Would Mr. Lincoln be willing to pay Mrs. Johnston's debts?

"What does that mean, Pa?" Abe said, when I finished reading and handed Pa back the letter.

"You don't know, Abe? Where's your smarts? It's plain as a wart on a hog. If I pay her debts, she will say yes."

"Why should you pay her debts?" I said boldly. "You don't have a lot of money, Pa, and you subscribed us to school, so—"

"Never you mind, Sally," he interrupted. "I got some

cash tucked away." He drummed his fingers on the table. "Sarah Johnston's a fine woman, a fine, sensible, hardworking woman. When your mama and I knowed her, we never seen her idle. It ain't no fault of hers that she's got debts. It's that worthless husband left her like that." He nodded to himself. "Yes, after your mother, Sarah Bush Johnston is as fine a woman as I ever would want to know."

"But she ain't Mama," I said, folding my arms across my chest.

"Don't get above yourself, Sally. Just listen here. I mean to marry her."

I turned away toward the fire to hide my face and my thoughts. *You can marry her, Pa, but she'll never be my mama.*

Abe looked at me, then he said, "You going to write another letter, Pa? You going to answer Mrs. Johnston's brothers? I can write it for you."

Pa shook his head. "Too much jawing, too many letters. I ain't got the time to waste. I'll talk to Sarah Bush Johnston and her brothers in person and get this business done."

"You're going to Kentucky?" Abe asked.

"Sure am."

"Me and Sally going with you?"

"I don't want to go," I said. I was still facing into the fireplace. "I'll stay right here."

"What's all that hard feeling in your voice, Sally?" Pa asked.

"Nothing," I said. I poked at the fire.

"All right, then," Pa said. "You and Abe are staying and taking care of the animals, and you can start going to school, too. Sally, are you listening to me, girl?"

"Yes, Pa," I mumbled.

"Well, turn around and let me see your face. If it don't snow the whole way to Kentucky, it won't be more'n three days going, three days to do my business, and three days coming back with your new mama."

CHAPTER 26

Good-bye, Pa

The morning he left for Kentucky, Pa shook me awake before the sun was up. He was dressed for travel. There was a dash to him that I hadn't seen before: his boots were oiled and his hat cocked. "You look real nice, Pa," I said, pushing aside the covers.

"Ain't going off like a ragged beggar with hat in hand, Sal."

Abe came down the ladder. "You going now, Pa?" he said, shoving the hair out of his face.

"Looks that way, don't it," Pa said.

I got up and packed meat and bread for the road for Pa, and Abe went out and saddled up Branch.

"There's a pig carcass hanging in the smoke shed," Pa said, when we went outside to see him off. "And plenty of meal and more to grind if need be."

"I know, Pa," I said.

"Don't forget, there's always neighbors, if need arises, but I don't want you to go running off the minute I'm out of sight. You hear me, Sal? You're in charge." He got up on Branch. "You know what has to be done. And you," he said to Abe, "there's the south field to clear of stones and plenty of wood splitting and fence building to keep you occupied. No idle hands. Good-bye, children," he said, and he rode out, the dogs yapping after him. "Hold back them dogs," he called.

Abe got the dogs and tied them to a stump.

"Good-bye, Pa," I yelled. And then it seemed as if every creature on the farm was yelling good-bye with me, the cows and chickens and hogs, all of them lowing and snorting around.

"Race you," Abe said, and we ran after Pa until he was out of sight.

When we got back to the cabin, Abe loosed the dogs and started in fooling with them, the way he never did when Pa was around. "Work, work, work," he chanted, and he ran round and round with the dogs, like he'd lost his mind.

"Abe, you fool! Stop that," I said. "Where's the wood for the fire? When you going to start clearing that field?"

Abe jumped up on a stump, his long skinny arms raised like a preacher's. "You will do the work of the Lord," he shouted. "By the sweat of your brow! All the days of your life! Get to work. Do your work, no idle hands."

"What are you waiting for, boy?" I was trying not to laugh. "Get to work."

"If you'll permit me one more word, Miss Sally-Worse-Than-Pa Lincoln. Work I must and work I will, but love it . . . *never*," he shouted and jumped down off the stump.

Pa weren't gone but three days when disaster come courting. Someone left the shed door unlatched. An animal broke in and carried away the pig carcass Pa had left us. That was all the meat we had.

"It was a bear," Abe said, showing me the tracks. "See that, Sally. Right there! Clear as day. Bear tracks."

"Must have been you that left it unlatched."

"No, it wasn't."

"I know it was you," I said. "I always latch the door."

"Me too!"

"Well, you didn't this time."

"Maybe it don't matter who did or didn't," he said. "It's done."

"What are we going to do now?"

"About what?"

"About food, fool!"

The dogs had been sniffing all around. Now they went barking and baying off, but they came back with nothing. "Useless critters," I yelled, and I threw a clod of dirt at them.

That night I made us stewed carrots and parsnips with the last piece of bacon which, lucky for us, hadn't been out in the shed. "I'm still hungry," Abe said, when we were done.

"I seen a flock of turkeys yesterday morning in the north field, Abe. Twenty-five of them, all fat and ready for roasting."

"I ain't going to kill them," he said.

"Why not?" I said it, but I knew what was coming. Abe was dead set against hunting, had been ever since he blew a turkey apart a while back when our cabin was fresh built.

"I ain't hunting," he said. "I gave it up."

"That don't make sense, Abe. We need meat, and turkeys are right out there, asking to be killed."

"No," he said. "I ain't doing it." He got that stubborn look on his face. "Can't never forgot how I turned something alive into a heap of bloody feathers."

"Maybe I'll take Pa's gun and do it myself."

"You don't know how to shoot, Sally. Pa never taught you."

"And that's too bad, ain't it! He should have."

"Maybe so," Abe said. "But *should have* don't help us get meat."

"Neither does *won't*," I shot back. "Guess we'll just have to be hungry till Pa gets here."

That was it for that night, but the next night, I went to where birds was roosting by the creek and knocked a bunch of them off the trees.

CHAPTER 27

I Make Friends

*M*onday morning, it was that blue-eyed boy-man, Aaron Grigsby, who brought us the news that school was starting on Wednesday, which was the first day of December. Aaron Grigsby didn't come on a horse this time, just his own two feet. And no rag on his head neither. He was wearing a coonskin hat, instead, like he was a mighty hunter.

"You aiming to go to the school?" he said.

"Why do you ask?" I was pinning up Abe's shirt that I had washed. My fingers were near frozen, but the sun was coming out and would soon dry it stiff.

"Just being neighborly. Me and my sisters are going."

"Don't mean I am." I knew I was being pert, but there was something about that boy that riled me up.

Wednesday morning, Abe and me were up early doing our chores, before we set out for school. I wrapped our lunch in a cloth and set it aside. Then I coiled up my hair careful, like Mama used to do, and pinned it with her horn comb. Maybe nobody would notice my patched dress.

The trees were swaying in the wind and a drift of snow covered the path. Abe was jumping around, hugging his books like they were living beings.

"Pa could be here when we come back from school today," I said. "He's been gone nine days."

"I hope he brings some game. I'm hungry for meat."

"He'll be bringing Mrs. Johnston and her brats; that's what he'll be bringing."

Abe looked at me. It was like seeing Mama's eyes on me. "Maybe she'll be nice, Sally."

"Could be," I grudged. "But I tell you what, Abe. When Mrs. Johnston comes, we're going to show ourselves the way Mama would want us to, standing straight and no wriggling. Letting her look and see what she got. See that she got a boy and a girl our mama would be proud of."

The dogs had run ahead, tails high, picking up the scent of animals and crossing back and forth and into the woods. All of a sudden, they came skittering and yelping back to us, their hair standing straight up and stiff. "They seen a bear or a panther," Abe said. We looked at each other and ran the rest of the way, but we were still late. When we got to the schoolhouse, smoke was busting out of the chimney and we could hear the class blabbing.

Abe went charging in and banged smack into the lintel. He had been growing so fast he didn't always know where his feet began or his head ended. To my mortification, his entering like that won us everyone's close attention.

It was dim inside, but light enough to see a fireplace at one end, three rows of benches divided down the middle, and the schoolmaster, Mr. Crawford, with his stiff whiskers, standing near his desk, holding a red-faced boy by the ear.

"'Morning, sir," I said. "I'm Sally Lincoln."

"You two sit down where you belong." He pointed Abe to the boys' side and me to the girls'. The girl I sat down next to had a nice dress and a green ribbon in her hair. She looked at me and wrinkled her nose. "How come your neck's so dirty?" she said and scooted away.

"Your neck ain't so fine," I said and, just for spite, I moved right up next to her.

"Euuuu," she cried, moving again, and almost fell off her seat.

"Katie Davis, quiet," the schoolmaster ordered. Then, to the boy he still had by the ear, he said, "Read."

The boy began. "'And . . . Israel said . . . said . . . unto . . . Jos . . . Jos . . . *Joseph* . . .'" He read as if he was stepping over hot coals, his voice squeaking up and down. "'. . . do not thy bre . . . breth . . . ren feed . . . the flock . . . in . . .'"

It were sure painful to hear! He croaked out a few more words and then the schoolmaster told him to sit and pointed his stick at Abe. "On your feet, Lincoln. Let me hear what you can do."

Abe stood up tall, took the book, and commenced. "'And Joseph went after his brethren and found them in Dothan. And they saw him afar off and before he came nigh to them they said one to another, "Behold the dreamer cometh," and they conspired against him to slay him.'"

I kept my eyes down, but I was proud as a peacock as my brother read. Smooth as cream! But not good enough for the master. "Too fast," he snapped. "Sit down."

Then it was my turn. I thought I would be shy, but turned out that I wasn't, not a bit. The master gave me a maxim to read. "'Our good or bad fortune depends greatly on the choice we make of our friends.'" I read it without stumbling. He had me read another maxim. "'Diligence, industry, and proper improvement of time are material duties of the young.'"

"Explain it."

"It means," I said, slowing down to get it right. "It means, don't shirk your duties, don't spend your time in idleness, and listen to your pa and mama." I sat down, wishing I had said listen to your *parents*. That would have sounded real fine.

Lunchtime, Abe and I ate together near the fire, but he was soon outside with the boys. I moved over to sit with the girls, and when I had something to say, I spoke up, even though the girl with the green ribbon kept whispering about me. I didn't care! I made friends with two sisters, Mollie and Nancy Pearce, Nancy being my age, Mollie being one year below us. Both of them had thick tangly hair as yellow as sunflowers.

"We like you, Sally Lincoln." Nancy said, "Don't we, Mollie?"

"Yes, we do," Mollie said.

"And Katie is a snob, isn't she, Mollie?"

"Yes, she is," Mollie said, and she patted my hand.

"And from now on," Nancy said, "we'll always eat lunch together."

"Yes, we will," Mollie said.

From that moment, I liked school.

*Y*ou'll be getting yourself a new mama soon," Katie Davis said the next day at lunch. She was wearing her hair in braids with a red ribbon tied on the end of each braid. "Maybe she'll make you wash up your neck." The other girls, all except Mollie and Nancy, giggled.

"I'm not getting no new mama," I said. "I got a mama already. I don't need a new one."

"Your mama's dead," Katie Davis said. "She's no good to you."

"Don't you say that!" I stood up right over her. I was ready to pull those red ribbons right off her head. "You take that back, Katie Davis. I don't care that my mama's passed. She's still my mama and the best one ever."

Nancy tugged me down. "Don't pay no attention to her," she said, and Mollie patted my hand.

Seemed like everyone knew Pa had gone off to Kentucky to court Mrs. Johnston. Some of the mamas sent their children to school with food for Abe and me. Those few days, we got stewed pears, corn dodgers, baked beets, and corn pudding.

"We don't need anything! We have plenty," I said, every time someone slid a bowl or package over to me.

"No, take it," Abigail Lewis said. "Mama says we got plenty, more than we need. You have to take it! She said, 'Don't come home with it.'"

Mr. Crawford heard us, and he decided to give the whole school a lesson on manners. "When giving," he instructed, pulling at his whiskers, "we say, 'Please accept this food. We have more than we need and want to share God's goodness.' Everyone repeat that."

He put his hand to his ear, and we all shouted it out, from big Jimmy Madison, who was going on eighteen and had a little beard, down to five-year-old Tory Winters.

"And when receiving," the schoolmaster said, "you must say, 'God bless your soul. Thank you for thinking of me.' And you young ladies could drop a curtsy as well."

That caused an explosion of curtsies and snickers, my snicker being the loudest and my curtsy the clumsiest. I didn't drop any more curtsies, either, even if I did take the food offered. Curtsies didn't seem real American to me!

Whatever food Abe and me carried away from the schoolhouse was gone before we were halfway home. Truth be told, we were hungry all the time since the bear had got our pig carcass. Saturday and Sunday seemed like the hardest days to get through. No extra food from the mamas and no schooling to take our minds off our stomachs. I got us some more birds, but it weren't near enough. When Monday came around, we were the first two pupils to arrive at the school. We were there even before the master.

CHAPTER 29

Waiting for Pa

By the time Pa had been gone two weeks, most mornings before we set out for school, I'd run out to the road to see if I could sight him coming along. When he left us, rain had been drenching down. Now snow was deep on the ground and long fat icicles dangled from the roof of the cabin. One morning, Abe got out to the road before me and came running back in, yelling, "I hear them! They're coming, Sal, they're coming."

I got all in a flurry and ran out barefoot, my hair uncombed, with Abe after me. There was no sign of Pa. There was no sign of anyone, not hide nor hair. "You fell for it, Sal," Abe said, slapping his knees like Pa did when he told a whopper.

"You devil!" I stomped back into the cabin. "I should thrash you good for tricking me."

"Sorry, Sal." He looked real penitent, but the next morning, he did the exact same thing. Came running in, all heated up, yelling, "I hear them! I hear them, Sal!"

And I fell for the same trick! That vexed me more than Abe's teasing, but when he tried it a third time, it didn't stir a hair on my head. He came running in, saying, "They're here, they're here."

I picked up my stirring spoon and said, "You go cover the wood stack with spruce, or you're going to feel this on your arse! I'm not jesting, Abe. Do it now, before we go to school."

"You sound like Pa," he said.

"I don't care!" I yelled. "If it was up to you, you wouldn't do nothing."

"That's what you say."

"Yes! That's what I say. Now git and do what I told you. I'm in charge here."

At the end of the day, coming home from school, the idea that Pa was in our cabin, with *her*, would sweep over me and I'd think of everything I'd neglected. "I didn't put the beans to soak, and I forgot to sweep out the cabin this morning."

"You didn't do the wash, either," Abe said.

"I hate doing it! It's a torment in this weather. She's going to think I'm lazy!"

"Don't matter what she thinks," he said. "You know

Pa's going to be peeved about something."

I started in running. "I don't want Pa and Mrs. Johnston waiting for us."

"There's nobody there," Abe said, trotting alongside me.

"You don't know that." Saying which, I ran straight into an overhanging branch and scratched up my face. "You don't know nothing," I screamed, mean as could be. "You're just a boy."

"And what do you think you are?"

"I'm the one who cooks and washes and takes care of you; that's who I am!"

He didn't say another word. Soon as we got home, the fire had to be built up, but Abe wasn't bringing in the wood, just kept looking for something to gnaw on. "There's nothing ever to eat around here," he said.

"How am I supposed to keep this fire going to cook, if you don't bring in wood. I'm hungry too!" The Devil came spilling out of my mouth. I had taken to bickering with Abe over everything. This waiting for Pa and his new wife was wearing me down. I said things I didn't ever want to say, called him slothful, lazy, worthless, things I'd heard Pa spit out that I had always hated.

Abe walked out. He was there, and then he wasn't. I sank down on a bench. "You're nothing like your mama,

Sally Lincoln," I said out loud, "and you never will be. I'm sorry, Mama, for being so bad."

I pulled a blanket over my shoulders and went outside, calling him. "Abe! Abraham! Abraham Lincoln! Abe, Abe, Abe!"

The sun was going down. I went around the pigpen and the barn and yelled his name some more. The dogs weren't around, so I said to myself they must be with Abe, and they wouldn't let anything happen to him. They'd fight off a bear, if need be. I kept calling his name, but then it started in snowing again, hard little flakes that stung. I got me an armful of wood and went back inside and built up the fire. Abe came shuffling in shortly after. Didn't look me in the face, just came over and stood by the hearth.

"Fire feels good, don't it?" I said. He didn't answer.

"I'll be cooking up some grits. Don't that sound good?" He didn't answer. "You're not talking to me?"

"I ain't eating tonight." He started up the ladder to the sleeping platform.

I went after him. "Abe, come on back here. I'm sorry I said those things. I didn't mean none of it. I swear I didn't."

He was halfway up the ladder. He turned and looked at me with a face that said he didn't care if I meant it or not.

"Come on down." I was about to lose my temper again with him. I went up the ladder and tugged on his overalls. "I didn't mean those words, not a one of them. You listening? You're the best brother a girl could have."

"What other brother you got?" he said.

"You're the only one I want."

"Huh!" he said, but he followed me down the ladder, and while I made the grits, he went out and brought in more wood and built that fire up into a blaze. That fire crackle was the best sound in the world, and that fire smell was the best smell.

We threw chestnuts into the fire, and later we went out and together carried in a backlog for the night. We lingered by the fire, talking about Aaron Grigsby and food and then about Pa and how long he'd been gone. Abe speculated some on the new mama coming our way. "Maybe she'll be fat and jolly like Aunt Betsy."

I didn't want to speculate one bit, but I didn't say anything. I let Abe's fancy carry him on. We were friends again, the way I knew our mama would want us to be.

CHAPTER 30

Missus Lincoln and Mister Grigsby

Without proper conversation," the master said, "you children are no better than pigs in the pen. Today, we're going to practice conversing."

He paired us, boy with girl, and instructed us to address each other as Mister and Missus and to carry on a pleasant conversation. Katie Davis was the first girl to go to the front of the room. She was paired with little John Jeffers. We all tried not to laugh as they conversed.

I was hoping to be paired with my brother, but to my mortification, when it was my turn, the master said, "Sally Lincoln and Aaron Grigsby, come to the front of the class."

Aaron Grigsby walked right up. He was wearing overalls and that blue rag tied around his neck instead of his head. He was one of the oldest boys in the class. He slouched, with his arms crossed on his chest. "Stand up straight, Grigsby," the master said. "Sally Lincoln, where are you?"

"Here I am," I said, standing up. He beckoned me to the front of the room. Aaron Grigsby and I faced each other.

"Go ahead, start," the master said. "Sally Lincoln, speak your piece. I see your mouth going all the time. Now, don't go timid on me."

I cleared my throat. "Uh, Mister Grigsby, uh, what work do you do, or are you a good-for-nothing idler?"

Mollie and Nancy giggled. Aaron Grigsby went a little red in the face, but he gave a fair answer. "I'm a farmer and a hunter, Missus Lincoln."

"And are you a hardworking farmer and a good hunter, Mister Grigsby?"

"Yes, I am, Missus Lincoln."

"And do you have fair and clear title to your land, Mister Grigsby, or do the rich folks back east own it?"

"I think it's my turn to ask you a question, Missus Lincoln."

"I'm waiting for your question, Mister Grigsby."

Everyone was laughing. "All right. Sit down," the master said, so I never did get to hear Aaron Grigsby's question.

The next day, we had a spelling bee. I was doing fine until I was given the word *beware*. My mind had been wandering, thinking about Aaron Grigsby, who was missing that day, and I left off the *E* at the end of the word.

"Shame, Sally," the schoolmaster said. "Sit down."

Pretty soon, Abe and little Mollie Pearce were the last two left standing. I knew Abe was going to be the spelling champion. Mollie got herself stuck on the word *defied*. She got the *D-E-F* part, and then she stood there, licking her lips and frowning. Abe put a finger to his eye and tapped as if he was rubbing soot out of it. After a moment, Mollie caught it and got the word right. Abe won anyway.

"Lucky for you, the schoolmaster didn't notice you giving Mollie that hint," I said on the way home, "or you would have got a birching. You wouldn't have been able to sit down for two days."

"I'd have to eat standing up."

"Might as well. We don't have that much to eat. Nobody brought us food today, and I'm hungry."

As if the Lord was listening to our grumbling, we found a whole mess of blue passenger pigeons laid out on our table. "Where'd they come from?" I said. They were all plucked and cleaned and ready to be roasted. "Maybe one of the neighbors brought them to us, maybe Mr. Little. God bless whoever it was."

I didn't waste no more time speculating. I got the fire hot and cooked those birds right up. Then we sat and ate them, every last one, down to their crunchy little bones, and then we chewed up the bones. We both slept good that night.

Next day, a mess of squirrel meat was waiting for us. "Who's doing this?" I said.

"I got a notion it's some feller living in the woods," Abe said.

"What kind of talk is that? You mean someone's squatting on our land?"

"No. I mean he's living in one of them hollow buttonwood trees."

"Quit your fooling. That's one of your whoppers."

"I saw him with my own eyes. Sunday, when I was out with the dogs. You know that buttonwood on the way to the creek, the one that's half-fallen over? I saw a feller dropping into the hole, like a squirrel into his nest."

"And I suppose you went in after him?" I said.

"I'm not daft. What if he was an outlaw or a smuggler? Could have been a whole gang of them inside that tree, it's big enough. I waited awhile, and then I crept up and stole a look."

"And what did you see, a mama raccoon with her pups? Or maybe a bear and her cubs?"

"Sally, I saw someone sitting in there, a man, snug, like he was sitting by his own fire."

"And who was he?"

"Too dark to tell. I believe he's the one who's been bringing us the game."

"And why would he do that? Just tell me, why would he?"

Abe couldn't answer that. If he wasn't lying, I figured we could leave it to Pa when he came home to find that feller. Unless Abe changed his story by then.

It was Friday evening and snowing when that Grigsby boy came to our door, all decked out like a mighty hunter, deerskin trousers and coonskin hat, a knife on his belt, and what he said was a wild pig slung across his shoulders. "I shot this here wild porker," he said. He was holding it by its feet. "It's for you and your brother."

I looked at the pig real close. "Abe," I said, "go count our pigs and come back and tell me if there's one missing."

"I believe you're being amusing," Aaron said.

"No, I'm not. Abe, go!"

Abe didn't move. Aaron smiled. "I'm taking no offense," he said. "Now, if you look closely, Sally Lincoln, you'll notice that this is not a fat corn-fed pig. Note how long and lean he is." He sounded like our schoolmaster, giving a lesson. "Note the scars and those tusks. This is an independent, self-sufficient, free-roaming pig. Sure as I'm standing in front of you, this here's a fighting pig. Before I shot him, he almost run me through."

Then he proceeded to butcher the pig, hang it from a limb, bleed it, and give me a gourd full of blood for pudding. "I'll secure that shed so the bear don't get in again," he said. He threw the guts to the dogs, who scrambled after them in a fighting pile.

I remembered Mr. Crawford's teaching, and said, "God bless your soul, Aaron Grigsby, for thinking of us."

I had a deep suspicion now who had left us those birds and squirrels, and there was nothing for it but to invite him to eat with us. Seeing as we had company, I made johnnycake, fried pumpkin, roasted corn, and heaps of pig meat that he'd shaved off the carcass, and everything out on our best trencher, the one Pa had made from a chunk of chestnut wood. By the time I sat down, I was almost too hot and sweaty to eat. I'm glad I did, though. That pig meat was good!

Aaron Grigsby was entertaining company. While we ate, he told us about the tiff he was having with his pa. "Ever since I came back from Kentucky, I made up my mind to stop sleeping with the rest of them. My pa don't like it, but there's ten of us in that cabin, plus the dogs, if they can squeeze in. It's worse than a den of wolves. My ma never wanted me to leave, but I told her I'd come visit her. And I told my pa it don't matter where I sleep, long as I show up to do my work every day. He don't want me to get schooling, either, so that's another reason I won't stay there. If I told him I was living in a tree, he'd likely go and burn it down."

"Sal, didn't I tell you?" Abe said. "Ain't it the giant buttonwood where you're sleeping, Aaron?"

He nodded. "But don't you say nothing about it to nobody."

"I wouldn't," Abe said. "Someday I might like to live like that, myself."

"Live in a tree?" I said. "And leave me? I won't allow it!"

Abe and Aaron laughed. Then Aaron said, "I didn't hear you say you won't tell no one where I'm living, *Missus* Lincoln."

"That's right," I said, "you didn't hear me say it, *Mister* Grigsby."

"But you won't, will you?" he said.

I took another piece of fry meat. I didn't say yes and I didn't say no. I figured I didn't have to answer that Grigsby boy nothing.

CHAPTER 31

Sinner Boy

All day Saturday snow was falling and falling and falling, thick heavy snow. You couldn't hear nothing with all that snow around, just sometimes an owl or the dogs barking. We stomped our way to the barn and the outhouse, and soon as we did, our footprints filled right up. Abe said we should tie a rope from the door to a tree by the path so if we had to go out at night we wouldn't get lost.

"I want you using the chamber pot," I said. And I gave him a severe look, so he'd know I meant it.

Sunday morning, as soon as I came plodding back from the outhouse, I made us some breakfast and then started in doing my chores. Brooming the floor first. That helped me think on things. It was *no* nine days since Pa had left for Kentucky. "Abe," I said. "You been counting the days Pa's been gone?"

"Nineteen," he said, almost before the words were out of my mouth. "Two more days, and it'll be full three weeks." He was setting on a stool, sharpening a whittling knife. "Maybe Pa ain't coming back."

"Bite your tongue," I snapped. The same wicked thought had traveled through my head. "It's sinful to think Pa would desert us."

"Then I'm a sinner, a sinner boy!" Abe got up and pulled on his overshirt. It had been Pa's until I had boiled the water too hot when I had washed it. Anyway, Abe was getting to be near as big as Pa, so it didn't fit him extra large.

"You going to help me neaten up this place?" I said, looking around at the mess.

"No. I'm going out."

"You going to romp in the snow, or are you going to work?"

"I'll milk Bessie and give the slops to the pigs."

"See that you do," I said.

"You sure are snappish this morning."

"I am not!" I screamed, and I threw the broom at him. He ducked through the door and slammed it closed.

Tears leaked down my cheeks, and I sat down on the

bench and then slid to the floor. What was the matter with me? I was the wicked one, not Abe. "Now, now, it's nothing, Sally," I said, pushing out the words, trying to sound like Mama.

I got up and found Amanda, where I'd tucked her underneath my mattress on the underbed. I held her up to my face and kissed her. "Do you think I'm wicked?"

'Course not.

I put her to stand on my outstretched legs. I held her arms. "Why am I always doing wrong, then, screaming and throwing things?"

Don't know, but you're sorry for it after, aren't you?

"Yes, real sorry."

That shows you're not wicked. Anyway, you'll be right as rain in another moment.

"That's what Mama would say."

I know. Are you going to tell Abe you're sorry?

"Yes! Soon as I see him."

Good, that's what Mama would want you to do. Are you okay now?

"Well, I was thinking, you know I'm near thirteen, I'm too old to play with dolls."

You're not playing with me, Sally! You're talking to me. You just tie me on your waist and go about your chores.

I did that, then I went to the window shutter and

shoved it aside. Snow was right up to the sill, but it had stopped falling, at last, and the sun was out. I raised my face to the warm, and it was like Mama's hand on my cheek.

Next I opened the door to let in the light. The dogs were right there, jumping and barking, trying to get past me. "Git down! No, you're not coming in." The two of them would have messed what little tidying I'd got done.

I built the fire and started mixing batter for corncakes. A good handful of cornmeal, another of flour, water, an egg, and a dab of molasses. The dogs were baying again. I stepped out. Their fur was all ruffed up and the little one, Samson, was growling deep in his throat. "Quit that yapping. What's got into you? And where's Abe?" I looked toward the path for my brother, and I saw what had got the dogs going.

A stranger dog, skinny and hungry looking, was loping down the path toward the cabin. Running behind him was a boy and a girl, both of them wrapped up good against the cold. I was so surprised I forgot my manners and instead of greeting them kindly, as Mama would have done, I called out in a harsh way, "Who are you?"

The girl stopped and stared at me, as if I'd scared her. She took a step back and said something to the boy that

I couldn't hear. "What?" I yelled. "What'd you say?"

"Are you Sally?" the boy said. "I guess you are, ain't you?"

Then I knew. Pa was back with Mrs. Johnston and her passel of children. Here were two of them, John and Matilda. Abe and I had talked and talked about the way we'd act when they came, but it wasn't supposed to happen this way, with Abe not here and me with a rag of an apron, Amanda tied around my waist, and a dripping spoon in my hand.

The skinny dog had gone around behind the barn, chased by Samson and Goliath, and the boy, John, went after them. The girl, Matilda, didn't move, just stood there picking at her shawl and staring at me. "Mama says we're to be sisters," she said. "Sisters. I have one sister. Um, my brother, too. He's nine." She nodded to herself. "Yes, he's nine. I'm ten."

"I know that," I said. "I'm older than you. I'm near thirteen."

"Oh." She kept picking at her shawl. "My mama and my new pa are coming." She nodded again. "They're coming."

"He's *my* pa," I said. "I've always had him. He's not *new*."

"Oh." She turned and looked behind her, and I heard the soft clop of horses' hooves in the snow.

CHAPTER 32

You Don't Have to Say Anything

$\mathcal{A}$ wagon, creaking and swaying under a heap of household goods and pulled by our Branch and a stranger horse, came into sight. At the same moment, Abe came pelting down the hill from the woodpile. "They're here," he said.

"I already saw Matilda and John. And their ugly dog," I added.

The wagon stopped and Pa dropped to the ground. He turned and held out a hand to a girl wearing a red cape and a red bonnet tied beneath her chin. "That must be Elizabeth," I said. "She looks like a city girl. She's so pretty!" My belly got all twisted up. I put my hands in my apron and rolled it up to my waist, but was that any better? My shift was sticky and spotted. I should have washed it and put it by the fire to dry.

Elizabeth gazed around and I heard her say, "Is this it? Is this your place, Pa? It's so . . ." She didn't finish, and Pa didn't say anything. He went around to the other side of the wagon to help a woman down. Her cheeks were raw red with cold.

It was *her*, Mrs. Johnston, wrapped in a black cape and with a frilled black bonnet on her head. She straightened and stretched and then wrapped her arms around herself and gazed all about, the way Elizabeth had done. "Well," she said in a thin high voice. "Well." Her face was bony and plain. She was nothing like our mama, who had been so fine and beautiful and who could make you cry when she lifted her voice in song.

Finally Pa looked around too and saw Abe and me standing by the cabin. "Come meet your new mama," he called.

I took Abe by the arm. "What are we supposed to say?" I whispered. We walked toward Pa.

"Come, children," Mrs. Johnston said, "come! Let me see you."

I stopped. I couldn't make myself take another step, but Abe went forward. He lifted his head and said, clear as day, as if he were a grown-up man, "I'm pleased to meet you."

I thought my heart would bust right out of my chest.

How could he say those words? He was lying! He wasn't pleased to meet her. He couldn't be! Not unless he'd forgotten our mama.

"And I'm so pleased to meet you, Abraham," Mrs. Johnston said. She looked Abe over, head to toe, and then she looked past him and did the same with me. Head to toe. "You poor things," she said. "You poor wild things. Those clothes! Well, never mind. I'm going to take care of you now." She stroked Abe's hair and called out, "Sally? Come, dear, let us get to know each other. Won't you come and take my hand?"

I didn't move. My hands were rolled up in my apron. I didn't take them out.

"Sally!" Pa said. "Go to your mama." It was an order.

I went to Mrs. Johnston, and I stood before her. She embraced me. She bent, and her head was close to mine. She didn't smell like Mama, she didn't sound like Mama, and she didn't look like Mama. She just wasn't Mama.

CHAPTER 33

Like Wild Animals

*W*ith Mrs. Johnston and Matilda and John and Elizabeth living in our cabin, everything was changed. Everything was different. When it was the way it was supposed to be—only Mama, Pa, Abe, and me—we were real comfortable. Our cabin was twenty by ten, just right for four people. Now with seven of us and their stools and trunks, you couldn't hardly breathe or take a step one way or another without bumping into someone or something.

At the table, we were all crowded so close, there weren't hardly room to lift your hand to your mouth. When Abe started right in to dip into the trencher, Mrs. Johnston called out, "Abraham!" and put her hand on his arm to stop him.

"We say grace before we eat, son. Didn't your
say grace?"

"Yes," Abe said, leaning back from the trencher. "Mama
always sang grace, but not—" He stopped, he didn't say
anything else, but I knew they all knew what he had left
out: . . . *but not Sally*.

For a little while after Mama had passed, I did try
singing grace the way she did, then I didn't do it no more.
Besides, morning and evening, I was always in a rush to
do my chores and not saying grace gave me a bit of extra
time. That's what I told myself anyway.

As if she caught what I was thinking, Mrs. Johnston
patted my hand and said, "I understand, dear."

She was a nice-talking lady, but there she sat in my
mama's place, with Pa saying *Mrs. Lincoln* to her, like
he used to do to Mama, and her three calling him Pa
and saying it so familiar, as if he was and always had
been *their* pa. When he came in from taking care of the
animals, John ran to him and Elizabeth patted the snow
off his shoulders. Seemed as if Pa favored them Johnston
young 'uns above Abe and me, too.

When we told him that we'd left the shed unlatched
and a bear had stolen the hog carcass, he give us both
harsh words for being so *careless*, so *stupid*, so *unworthy*
of his trust. I knew we deserved those words and maybe

a whipping, but it was hard that he spoke so meanly to us and so kindly to Mrs. Johnston's three. Never an ill-tempered word, not even when John lagged so bringing in the wood that the fire near went out.

Food changed too. Mrs. Johnston had her own way of cooking. Everything she made was more salty and sugary than Mama's way. Not that it was evil tasting, but I weren't used to it, and I surely favored Mama's cooking over hers. Sometimes I didn't even want to eat a bite.

Then she would look at me and say, "Sally? I want you to eat, child." She had that thin high voice, gentle enough, but like a bee sting to me. Sharp and quick. "Are you feeling poorly?" she'd say. "Could you sit a little straighter, dear? Don't you know it's good for your health to keep a straight back?"

Those weren't her only questions to me. She wanted to know had I laid hay around the henhouse to protect the hens from the cold, and how were the hens laying, and had I been collecting the eggs every day? Well, I hadn't been, with so many chores and school and Abe to think about, but she said it was neglectful, and such a shame, so much waste!

"Well, never mind," she said. "Elizabeth can be in charge of the henhouse from now on."

Even sleeping and sleeping places changed. First off,

each of her children kissed her good night, and she said me and Abe were to do it too. Abe went right up, but Pa had to speak sharp to me. I suppose I should have been glad I had to sleep upstairs with Elizabeth and not near her mother. But I weren't glad to give up the underbed. I had to, though, because, plain and simple, Matilda was scared of everything.

She was more'n a year older than John, but she was scared of mice, scared of fire, scared of the sleeping platform and the woods and trees and wild animals and strangers and ghosts and spirits, and the dark. Most especially, the dark. That's why she had to sleep near her mama. "I always sleep near my mama," she said. That's why she got the underbed, and I was climbing the ladder to the sleeping platform. I wouldn't have minded if it was Abe and me, like it used to be, but it was me and Elizabeth in one bed and Abe and John in the other.

First night, soon as we'd said our prayers and crawled into bed, Elizabeth started sniffing the air. "What's that smell?" she said. "What do I smell?"

"What smell?" I said. "I don't smell nothing."

"A rat never smells its own hole," she said, and pinched her nose.

I didn't have a word to say back. It just put me in mind of school, first day, when Katie Davis had called me dirty. Except, now, there was no Mollie to pat my hand and no Nancy to tell me Elizabeth was a snob and pay her no attention.

John and Abe had the other bed, and that night and for the next few nights, they scrambled something fierce over the quilt they had to share, yanking and pulling it between them and smacking their legs into each other and snorting and huffing like a couple of donkeys.

"You boys stop that," Elizabeth said, "or I'll come over and thrash you both." She reared up and turned over so hard, she near shoved me out of the bed! I clung on to the edge and let her take up most of the place. I sure didn't want to sleep close on her.

Elizabeth did that sniffing the next night too. And then she started in whispering, "Sally, Sally. You know what my mama said when she saw you standing there in the doorway that Sunday we come here? She said you and Abraham didn't hardly look human, looked like animals."

I thrashed my arms around. "Your mama didn't say that!"

"Yes, she did. That's what she said."

"I don't believe you, Elizabeth Johnston!" Even if I didn't want her mama to be mine, I knew her mama weren't a mean person.

But then . . . I heard her! I heard her saying it! It was later that night, and I woke up and lay there, listening to the boys snoring in their sleep and hearing whispering downstairs. I got out of bed and used the chamber pot, and that was when I heard it.

I heard her saying, "Broke my heart, Mr. Lincoln, your young 'uns looking like wild animals."

So Elizabeth wasn't lying! My heart got set hard against her mama and all of them. And maybe it got a little hard against Abe, too. He and John were making friends. They still fought over the quilt every night, seeing which one of them could best the other, but they liked doing it. And John didn't mind that Abe usually won. He said Abe was his big brother, and he had always wanted a big brother. So whatever Pa set Abe to doing, John was doing it with him. They whispered together and laughed. They had secrets and wouldn't tell me anything. Abe didn't hardly talk to me no more.

CHAPTER 34

Pretty Is As Pretty Does

I still had chores, we all did, but now Mrs. Johnston did the most of it. She was getting into all the corners of the cabin with her rag and broom. She even climbed up the ladder to the sleeping platform. "We'll have to give this a good cleaning," she said. She sniffed the way Elizabeth had, but she didn't hold her nose.

"I want you two to hang out the bedclothes to freshen," she said, "and then you must scrub the floor."

Elizabeth made a face at me. She and her mama were always together, fixing food and cleaning and washing and sewing. She didn't like that she had to do something with me, and when we were toting the bedclothes down the ladder, she said so.

"I don't like it, neither," I said, quick as a shot. "I could do this alone."

"Oh, be quiet," she said. "My mama said for us to do it, and you got to do what she says."

We tussled over putting that stuff on the line, too. She said I was dragging the quilts in the snow. I pulled them one way; she pulled the other. It's a mercy that we ever got them hung right. Later, her mama sent us to take them in. Then she had us hold them, one at each end, and warm them by the fire before we brought them back up to the sleeping place.

What with all the cleaning and arranging, it was some many days before Mrs. Johnston got all her goods unpacked. When she did, she gave Abe a book, which set him afire. He went prancing around, clutching that book like it were gold. I thought she didn't have nothing for me, but she pulled out a dress from her trunk and gave it to me. It was blue and white gingham, with a white collar and six buttons. It was finer than anything I'd ever had. I stuck my hands into the sleeves and pulled the dress over my head.

Mrs. Johnston fussed with the collar. "It's a hand-me-down from your sister Elizabeth," she said. "You might as well get some use out of it. It will be some while before our Matilda fits into it." She smoothed the dress down and stood back, her hands on her waist. "Why, there! Fits you like a glove, and look how pretty you are."

Nobody had ever called me pretty. Mama always said,

"Pretty is as pretty does." She had no use for fussing, but maybe Mama didn't need to fuss. She was naturally beautiful. When I went up to the spring for water, I twisted this way and that to see my reflection. Was I pretty? Was I? How I wished I could ask someone if it were the truth!

"What are you doing?" Matilda said. She was always saying everything two times. "What are you doing, Sally?"

"I'm getting the water, Matilda."

"Why are you making funny with your head, Sally? Why are you making funny with your head?"

John was the youngest, but Matilda was more like the baby. Her mama petted her and excused her from work. She was scared even of the chattery little chickadees that came to the spring.

All day, I kept hearing those words. *Look how pretty you are!* At the table that night, I found myself looking on Mrs. Johnston with more favorable eyes. I even liked it when she leaned over toward my brother and said in her high quiet voice, "Abraham. It's unsightly to chew with your mouth open, son."

Abe looked at her, his eyes widening. "Oh." He clamped his mouth shut and chewed hard on the piece of meat he'd speared.

"Abe," Pa said. "Did you hear your mama speaking to you?" Now Pa was also leaning toward him. Big as he was, Abe looked small between them. He nodded and chewed and swallowed. "Then answer your mama," Pa said.

"Pa! He did answer."

"I weren't talking to you, Sally."

"But, Pa—"

"Sally, sew up your mouth, unless you want me to do it for you. Is that what you want?"

"No, Pa." Next to me, Elizabeth turned her head and frowned, as if she was the mama.

"Now, Abe," Pa went on, "we aim to have manners here. Your mama likes manners, and when she talks to you, you don't say, 'Oh.' You say, 'Yes, Mama.'"

Your mama likes manners. As if our real mama didn't like manners!

"You hearing me, boy? I don't want to slap your head to make you remember."

"Mr. Lincoln, there's no need for that," the new mama said. Pa was glowering, but she went right on. "I've prepared a surprise for you all. Something John is real partial to at this time of year when the apples are getting low and soft."

"Apple crisp," John shouted out. "Do you like that, Pa?"

"Ain't had any of that for a long time," Pa said. He licked his lips.

She brought the black pan to the table and dolloped out two big chunks for Pa and smaller ones for us. We all watched while he took the first bite. "Good!" he said. "Good! Thankee, Mrs. Lincoln."

In bed that night, I folded my hands on my chest and closed my eyes. I was thinking about Mama, wondering if I ever heard Pa saying 'thankee' to her.

Elizabeth poked my shoulder. "You sleeping, Sally? I don't mind that Mama gave you my old dress. I was growing right out of it. Anyway, I have three dresses."

"*Three!*" I couldn't help repeating it.

"My mama says we may be poor, but she's not going to have her girls looking like church mice, like some do."

I turned over, away from her, clinging to the edge of the bed again.

CHAPTER 35

One Family

School was going on through January and February, but Pa said he didn't have the cash money to send all of us to school, especially for all that time. "You and Abe had your turn," he told me. "And your mama needs Elizabeth. John and Matilda can go in January."

"Why do you have to send them, Pa? Abe wants to go to school! And me, too. You know we want to go, Pa."

"Quit your jawing at me, Sally. We're going to give the other children their turn. Didn't I say that they're mine now, just like you and Abe? We're one family now."

That's what they all said. One family. I was the only one who didn't think it or say it.

Along about that time, Matilda took to following me around. I suppose it were a natural thing. Her sister was always with her mama and her brother with Abe. The way I saw it, we were the only two not hitched up. Besides, my stepmama liked that Matilda was after me. She sure weren't no help in the cooking or cleaning, always getting in the way as Elizabeth and her mama scurried about. Then my stepmama would say, "Matildy, sweets, go and study your letters . . . help Sally peg up the wash . . . don't Sally need help slopping the pigs?"

When she wasn't in school, Matilda was trailing me. I went to the woodpile, and there she was. I went out to the barn, same thing. I went to the spring with the pails, didn't even hear her following me. I turned around, and there she was. "What do you want?" I said. Same thing I said every time.

"Nothing." She twisted her braid. "Nothing." She said that every time.

"You're always behind me." She nodded. "All right, then, you can carry one of the pails."

"I will do it." She was a skinny little bit. She had to pick it up with two hands. "I'm not strong like you," she said.

"I'm strong like my mama."

"Your mama's in heaven now. My mama's here, not in heaven."

"Don't talk so much. You'll tip that bucket and spill all the water."

"I won't!" She made an awful face and held on to it.

Lots of days, Matilda had a sore head or a sour stomach and she didn't go to school. Then Abe took her place and went off with John, and she was after me all day. One morning, when she was staying home, she came tagging after me to the spring. "Sally," she said, in her little voice, "I'm scared."

"What are you scared of now?"

"I have to recite a poem for the master. I have to recite it."

"That's nothing to be scared of." I dipped the pail.

"I won't be good," she said. "I'll forget. I know I won't be good."

"Yes, you will be," I said. I started down the path. "Say that poem for me. Come on." I put down the pail and took her by the hands and looked severely in her face. "Now, say it."

In a quivering voice, she started, "'Had a mule, his name was Jack.'" She stopped. "I forgot." Her face crumpled. "I always forget. The master will hit me."

"'Rode his tail to save his back,'" I said. "Now you say it." She did. "Good. What's next?" She shook her head, looking real mournful. "Listen. I'll say it, then you say it. 'His tail got loose and I fell off. Whoa, Jack!'"

I made her repeat it. We did that and did that, until

she could recite it straight through. "'Had a mule, his name was Jack. Rode his tail to save his back. His tail got loose and I fell off. Whoa, Jack!'"

"Very good," I said.

"Is it very good?"

"Yes!" I picked up the pail. "When the master calls on you, you go up in front and pretend you're saying it to me."

Next day, when she went off to school with John, she was mumbling the rhyme to herself. Strange thing, I kept thinking on her all day. When she came home, she ran to me, hugged me around my waist, and said, "I did it. I did it, Sally. I did it!"

"'Course you did," I said, and I patted her head real gentle.

CHAPTER 36

Corncake Crumbs

$\mathcal{I}$n late February, Cousin Dennis came riding back on Lightning. He said he favored us, he favored our company. He favored working with Pa and living with us. After the evening meal, we were all together. Often, Abe read to us from the Bible or from the storybook he was reading. Our stepmama had given him two more books, and sometimes he read to her from one or the other while she was spinning.

It were still troublesome to me to call her Mama, but not to Abe. He took to loving her as much as our own mama, and that grieved me. But we were both older now, me thirteen and Abe eleven, and I didn't chastise him on that account. He was close on being a man. He could do a man's work any day.

Dennis made his sleeping place in the half shelter and sometimes Abe and John went and slept out there with him too. On those nights, especially, Matilda would climb up and sleep in the bed with me and Elizabeth, tuck herself right between us. She'd wriggle around to get comfortable, and then hug me and kiss me, too. Kiss my hand and then my cheek, and say, "Kiss me back, Sally! Your turn. Kiss me back."

After a while, Elizabeth would stop pretending to be asleep and sit up and say, "Give me a hug here, Matildy. Hug your big sister! And I want some kisses, too."

Matilda would hug her right off, hug and kiss her, and we would all be playful, but Matilda would always tuck her hand into mine for sleeping. One night, after we settled down, Elizabeth took Matilda's other hand, and we went to sleep like that, lying three in a row and holding hands. Come the morning, we woke up like that, too! It made us all laugh.

"Had it been the boys," Elizabeth said, "they couldn't have stayed still in one place for more'n two minutes."

"But not us girls," Matilda said.

And almost at the same moment, Elizabeth and I both echoed, "Not us girls!"

April came and everything was warming up, the snow starting to melt and the sky more blue than gray. It was a glad time. One morning I pocketed some of my corncake, and when it was time to go to the spring, I called Matilda to come along. It was washing day, and we had three pails to carry. "I'm going to show you something," I said as we walked up the hill.

At the spring, I dipped the pails and handed them to Matilda to put aside. Then I led her to the edge of the woods to show her the little yellow flowers of the coughwort. "See that?" I said. "It's got more names, but coughwort is the name my mama told me. My mama made a healing tea from the leaves. If you had bad lungs or a cough, she would give it to you and you'd soon be better."

Matilda knelt down and plucked one of the little yellow flowers and stuck it in her braid. "What else?" she said. I showed her the tiny salt-and-pepper plant and violets, which she knew, and bloodroot. "What else?" she said again, so we went farther into the woods and sat down on a fallen tree in a clearing.

I took out my corncake and crumbled it on the palm of my hand. "What are you doing?" she said.

"Wait. You'll see."

Soon a flock of the little chickadees appeared and flew

around us, chattering. One landed on my hand, pecked a crumb, and flew off. Then another landed so lightly I hardly felt it, and another, and another. Each one pecked a crumb and flew into the trees.

"I'll do it," Matilda said. She held out her hand, and I put corncake crumbles in it. A bird landed on her palm with its tiny black feet. "Oh, oh!" she cried, and yanked her hand back, spilling all the crumbs. But at once she put her hand out again. I gave her the rest of the corncake. Her hand shook as the birds landed, but she kept it stretched out until every crumb was gone.

"That was brave, Matilda," I said.

After that, near every time we went to the spring together, we had to find the little flowers in the woods and go to our secret clearing and call the birds to us with corncake crumbs.

≫⁓ C H A P T E R 3 7 ⁓≪

A Bright Kindness

September was the birth month for Elizabeth and Matilda, and Pa said he wanted to give them a fair treat. He got out the wagon, loaded it with hay, and hitched up Branch. Elizabeth, Matilda, Abe, and John all climbed on for the ride. Our stepmama said she would stay home and cook up a special meal.

"Get on, Sally," Matilda called. She was bouncing up and down.

"Come on, Sally," my brother said. "It won't be no fun without you."

I started toward the wagon, then I stopped. Something was hurting my heart. We hadn't never had a festive time for me and Abe, nor for Mama, neither.

"I'll stay," I said.

Pa called out, "Gee'up, Branch!" And away they went off. They were all singing.

I followed my stepmama back into the cabin. We worked together for some time. "Sally, dear, are you feeling ill?" she asked.

"No." I didn't look at her.

"Well. It's such a lovely day. We'll sit outside and rest ourselves."

We went out and sat down on the stone, the one Mama never saw, near the lilac bush. Little as it were, it had burst out with blossoms in May. "You planted that bush, didn't you?" my stepmama said.

"Yes."

"I'm so glad. A lilac bush belongs right by the dooryard."

"My mama wanted it bad," I said, "but she never got to see it. Never got to smell those flowers."

My stepmama patted my head. "Maybe she did, from heaven."

"No," I said, "she didn't! You're wrong. She never got to see it here, or in heaven, or anywhere." I started crying.

"Why, Sally . . . Sally dear," my stepmama said. "What is the matter?"

"It's my mama," I sobbed. "She gave up so much when we left Kentucky, her home and neighbors and church regular, and baby Thomas's grave. And she never complained, never a cross word to Pa, and always gentle and nice with me and Abe. And what did she get? Nothing. She got *nothing*."

"Oh, Sally, it's not so. She had you."

"Me?" I bent over my knees, sobbing. "I weren't even a good daughter."

"Of course you were. You loved her; you were a good daughter to her. I know that for a fact. I know that!"

"How do you know that?" I lifted my head but I didn't look at her.

"I know because I know you. You have a good heart, Sally. I *know* you were a loving daughter, a good daughter. Do you know, darling, what that's worth to a mama? It's priceless. A mama who has that, has everything." She took me by the chin and dabbed my cheeks with her apron.

In all these months, I'd always looked away when she spoke to me. Now I looked at her, full in the face, and I saw the same bright kindness for me in her eyes that I always saw for her own children and for my brother. She began humming and put her arms around me. Slowly I lowered my head and let it rest against her breast. She smelled like fresh-baked bread. Slowly I put my arms around her waist and moved closer.

Later, when they all came home, John and Matilda pelting into the house, Abe busting to talk about their wagon ride, and Elizabeth coming behind, my stepmama and me were laughing over some trifle and I was pulling a pan of shortbread out of the fire.

AFTERWORD

In 1779, while the American Revolution was going on, the first Abraham Lincoln crossed from Virginia to Kentucky on foot, in a group of about a hundred people led by Daniel Boone. He was accompanied by his wife, Bathsheba, and five children. One of them was a toddler named Thomas, who was destined to be the future father of Sarah and Abraham Lincoln. When Thomas was six years old, he saw his father, who was clearing land in the forest, killed by the Indians. An older brother saved him from captivity. He began working at that young age and had virtually no education.

We know less about Nancy Hanks's background. We know that she was born on February 5, 1784, possibly in Campbell County, Virginia, or possibly in Hampshire County (now Mineral County), West Virginia. When Nancy was nine, her father died. Her mother, apparently a young girl without means, brought Nancy to her sister and brother-in-law, the Richard Berry family, with whom she lived until she was married. Nancy's first cousin Sarah Mitchell, who had been taken by the Indians when she was five or six, also lived with the Berry family after her release from captivity at the age of twelve. The two young girls became very close.

Nancy Hanks and Thomas Lincoln were married on June 12, 1806. Eight months later, their first child, Sarah, was born in Elizabethtown, Kentucky. We know very little about Sarah "Sally" Lincoln. We do know that she was named Sarah after her mother's "sister-cousin" Sarah Mitchell. We know she was married at the age of nineteen on August 2, 1826, to Aaron Grigsby, a neighbor of the Lincolns', and we know that she died in childbirth on January 20, 1828, at the age of twenty-one.

All else, her entire life, the reality of her, a young girl in a family destined for fame because of her younger brother, is virtually unknown. John Hanks, a cousin on her mother's side, is quoted as having said of her that she was kind, "tender, and good natured and . . . smart."

Within the confines of historical facts about the Lincoln family—when they moved from the Knob Creek farm in Kentucky to their holding on Pigeon Creek, in what became the state of Indiana, when and how Nancy Hanks Lincoln died, and when Thomas Lincoln and Sarah Bush Johnston were married—within those confines, I have imagined the life and personality of Sarah Lincoln, this unknown girl who died so young.

Nancy Hanks Lincoln, Sally's mother, died of poisoning caused by white snakeroot, a plant then abundant in Indiana territory. After cows ate snakeroot, they developed the "trembles" and within three days, they were dead. Although the illness was called "milk sickness," it was not known that cows ate this weed and passed on the poison, tremetol, in their milk. The water supply was suspected of somehow being contaminated, and many farms were abandoned as people fled for their lives.

Although Abraham Lincoln rarely talked about his sister, it was known that they had been close. He was also affectionate and devoted to his stepmother, Sarah Bush Johnston, a warmhearted woman, whom Abe looked after in her old age. However, when he left home at the age of twenty-one, he may never have seen his father again and did not even attend his funeral.

GLOSSARY

backlog: a log against which a fire is built

bannock: unleavened cake made of cornmeal, baked next to the fire

bulls foot: plant used as an herbal remedy for respiratory illnesses

chamber pot: a vessel used for elimination during the night

corn dodger: a form of corn bread; also called corn pone; also called johnnycake

coughwort: a common spring plant known by many names, for example, coltsfoot and horsefoot

pawpaw: small woodland tree and its fruit native to eastern United States

sweep: the long-handled oar used to propel and steer a raft or boat

tow: coarse flax fiber prepared for spinning

trace: a trail through a forest